Llywelyn
AP GRUFFUDD

Llywelyn
AP GRUFFUDD

The Life
and Death
of a
Warrior
Prince

Peter Gordon Williams

Cover design: Olwen Fowler / Thinkstock

ISBN: 978 1 78461 139 2

Published and printed in Wales
on paper from well-maintained forests by
Y Lolfa Cyf., Talybont, Ceredigion SY24 5HE
e-mail ylolfa@ylolfa.com
website www.ylolfa.com
tel 01970 832 304
fax 832 782

Dedicated to the memory of my wife Jean

"*O for the touch of a vanish'd hand*
And the sound of a voice that is still.
The tender grace of a day that is dead
Will never come back to me."

Tennyson

Characters

WELSH ROYAL HOUSEHOLD

Llywelyn ap Gruffudd	*Prince of Wales*
Llywelyn ap Iorwerth	*Llywelyn's grandfather*
Owain	*Llywelyn's brother*
Dafydd	*Llywelyn's brother*
Rhodri	*Llywelyn's brother*
Eleanor	*Llywelyn's wife*
Gruffudd ap Llywelyn	*Llywelyn's father*
Einion ap Caradog	*Llywelyn's uncle*
Dafydd	*Gruffudd's brother*
Tegwared	*Gruffudd's brother*

SUPPORTERS

Iorwerth ap Gwrgunan	*A lord of Perfeddwlad*
Tudor ap Madoc	*A lord of Gwynedd*
Dafydd Benfras	*Court Poet*
Matthew Paris	*Poet and Chronicler*
Maredudd ap Rhys Gryg	*Later turned traitor*
Maredudd ab Owain	*A lord of Deheubarth*
Gruffudd ap Madog	*A lord of Powys Madog*
Gruffudd Fychan	*Gruffudd's son*
Gwion of Bangor	*Emissary to Scotland*
Simon de Montfort	*Earl of Leicester*
Amoury	*Montfort's son*
Guy	*Montfort's son*
Henry	*Montfort's son*

Simon	Montfort's son
Nicholas Seagrave	Military Commander
Goronwy	Llywelyn's steward
Morgan	A Welsh thrall
Alexander III	King of Scotland
Alan of Irvine	Scottish emissary

OPPONENTS

Henry III	King of England
Edward	Henry's son
Richard	Duke of Cornwall
Stephen of Bauzan	Military Commander
Rhys Fychan	Later joined Llywelyn
Humphrey de Bohun	Earl of Hereford
Gilbert de Clare	Earl of Gloucester
Geoffrey de Langley	Edward's Steward
Gilbert Talbot	Justice of Chester
Reginald de Grey	Justice of Chester
Roger Lestrange	Marcher Lord
James Audley	Marcher Lord
Roger Mortimer	Marcher Lord
Roger	Mortimer's son
Edmund	Mortimer's son
Luc de Tany	Military Commander
Hywel ap Meurig	Constable of Cefnllys

CLERGY

Bishop Anian	
Archbishop Kilwardby	
Archbishop Pecham	
Cardinal Ottobuono	The Pope's emissary
John of Wales	

ICONS LLYWELYN ADMIRED

Hywel Dda	*A 10th-Century Welsh Prince*
Saint David	*Patron Saint of Wales*
Giraldus Cambrensis	*Scholar and Writer*
Harold Godwinson	*Last Saxon King*

LEGENDARY

Aeneas	*A nobleman of Troy*
Brutus	*Aeneas' great-grandson*
Ignoge	*Brutus' wife*
Latinus	*King of Italy*
Turnus	*King Rutuli*
Assaracus	*An ally of Brutus*
Pandrasus	*King of the Greeks*
Antigonus	*Pandrasus' brother*
Anacletus	*Antigonus' friend*
Corineus	*An ally of Brutus*
Goffar the Pict	*Ruler of Aquitaine*
Gogmagog	*Leader of the Giants*

PROLOGUE
The hidden future

THE DAY WAS shading into dusk when a lone horseman appeared on the bridle path. Although the sounds of battle – the ring of sword on helm, the neighing of terrified horses and the dismal cries of dying men – had faded into silence, the prince's appearance – shattered shield hanging on a bloodied arm, broken lance lying uselessly across the saddle horn and an empty scabbard flapping against the horse's flank – bore witness to the carnage that had taken place on a battlefield so very near.

The rider's gentle progress was halted when a knight in full armour, mounted on a great black stallion, suddenly appeared and blocked his path. The knight lowered his lance and charged full tilt at the defenceless prince. The point of the lance pierced the prince's breastplate and catapulted him off his horse and onto the ground where he lay with arms extended as if in supplication. Blood trickled from his open mouth and he died with a look of mild surprise on his face. The knight, unaware of the status of his victim, rode off into the gathering gloom. This chance encounter destroyed the hopes of a nation.

CHAPTER 1

The end of an era

M Y GRANDFATHER, LLYWELYN ap Iorwerth, suffered a stroke and repaired to Aberconwy Abbey to recuperate. When he died some months later, I thought back to the days of my childhood spent in the royal court of Llywelyn ap Iorwerth, Prince of Gwynedd. He chose the title 'prince' to ensure that the concept of a principality would be used in official records, thus ensuring the integrity of a Welsh nation.

I had three brothers – the eldest was Owain, while Dafydd and Rhodri were my younger brothers. We all stood in awe of our warrior grandfather who, by force of arms and political persuasion, had attained a dominant position among the squabbling lords who ruled the warring realms of Wales. I sensed that, because we both had the same first name, he favoured me above his other grandchildren,

Llywelyn was acutely conscious of the contempt in which the English on the other side of Offa's Dyke viewed the Welsh, believing we were a race of uncultured, bloodthirsty barbarians. I will always remember that day when he called me to his side and pressed my head to his chest. I can still feel the roughness of his woollen tunic against my face, as he spoke passionately of the history of our ancestors. He told of the kingdom of Brycheiniog and of the vast lake that lay within its confines.

Its ruler commissioned an architect from Ireland to build an artificial island in the centre of the lake. This was done by driving wooden stakes into the bed of the lake and building up a platform of brushwood and rubble to above the water level. The resulting island is known as a crannog, and on this structure the king built his palace. He furnished it with tapestries and furniture from all over the known world and he dressed his queen in fabrics from lands far to the east.

At that point, Llywelyn cupped my face in his hands and staring hard into my eyes said, 'Does that king strike you as being a barbarian?'

I answered, 'No, grandfather. But what happened to the crannog?'

'The real barbarians came over the dyke and destroyed everything.'

Llywelyn claimed to have traced his lineage back 300 years to the 10th century and Hywel Dda, a prince whose power base was Deheubarth in south-west Wales. From there he extended his power over Gwynedd and other parts of Wales. His greatest legacy was the codification of Welsh laws, which defined a separate Welsh identity. Like all Welsh princes before him, he was required to submit to the jurisdiction of the English crown, which he did and, as a result, Hywel Dda died peacefully in bed rather than on a blood-soaked battlefield.

My grandfather also spoke eloquently of other icons of Welsh history. Saint David born in the 6th century, the details of whose life were obscured by the intervening years. In 1009 a Welsh scholar, Rhygyfarch, ventured where others failed to tread and wrote a biography of the saint, that was littered with unauthenticated facts. He boldly asserted that David's conception was inauspicious and had occurred when the King of Ceredigion raped a nun. David was educated at Henfynyw and, on taking holy orders, he was prominent in suppressing the Pelagian heresy that denied the doctrine of original sin.

He founded numerous churches throughout south Wales and moved the seat of ecclesiastic government from Caerleon to Mynyw. For the people of Wales, Saint David represented early Christianity and national unity.

Another man whom Llywelyn respected was a near contemporary of his, Giraldus Cambrensis. Of noble birth, Giraldus was born in 1146 at Manorbier castle and was educated in Paris. On returning to Wales he was appointed Archdeacon of Brecknock. He entered the service of King Henry II in July 1184 and, as a result of two journeys he made on the king's behalf, he wrote two highly regarded books on Ireland and Wales. He left the king's service in 1195 and retired to Lincoln to study theology.

Throughout his life he nursed a desperate ambition to become Bishop of Saint Davids and secure its independence from Canterbury. This unfulfilled ambition led him to reject four Irish and two Welsh bishoprics. He wrote his autobiography in 1206 and resigned his archdeaconry a year later. He died at the age of seventy-seven years, a symbol of culture and patriotism.

There was one surprising figure in my grandfather's pantheon, Harold Godwinson, Earl of Wessex, who became the last Saxon to rule Britain. During the first half of the 11th century, King Edward the Confessor sat on the throne but it was Harold who exercised the power.

In 1055 a dispute arose between Earl Alfgar, son of Leofric, Earl of Mercia, and Harold's brother, Tostig, over the possession of Northumbria. The conflict resulted in Alfgar being outlawed and he fled to Wales where he made an alliance with Gruffudd, a prince of Gwynedd, giving his daughter Aldyth in marriage to the Welsh leader. News came that Harold, after being cursed during a hunting expedition by a wild Welsh witch, had taken to his bed and was too weak to rise from it. Alfgar saw this as his opportunity to exact revenge on the Godwin family. He and Gruffudd, with an army consisting mainly of Welshmen, laid waste the city of Hereford, making great slaughter. They then rampaged at will throughout the March, spreading death and destruction in their wake. With Harold confined to his bed by a seemingly incurable illness, the pair were not expecting any serious resistance. Imagine their surprise when a vast army appeared over the horizon and made camp in a field near Cheltenham. Anxious to determine the composition and intentions of this formidable array of armed men, Alfgar summoned Gil, an Irish minstrel in his service, and sent him as a spy into the enemy camp. Gil sang to his harp as he wandered among the men gathered around their campfires. He heard talk of Harold's witch-induced illness that had prevented him being there to lead his army into battle. Suddenly, there was a great stirring among the men as five magnificently caparisoned horsemen galloped into the camp and drew up before the pavilion. The soldiers rose to their feet and ran to gaze in awe at the scene that was developing. There, with two housecarls on each side, Harold Godwinson sat astride his white charger, with a warrior's cloak over his shoulders. In his right hand he gripped a blue standard with a golden cross.

The men called out excitedly, 'Earl Harold, Earl Harold.'

Harold raised his hand and said, 'Saxons all. But two days ago, I lay helpless on my bed beyond the help of the most learned doctors. Then two humble priests made offerings at that modest shrine Waltham Holy Cross. Soon hundreds of my followers did the same and beseeched our Good Lord Jesus to confound the evil spell cast on me and restore me to complete health and vigour. You see the result.'

The men gave a great hurrah and, raising their swords, shouted in unison, 'Tomorrow, we go into battle led by our Golden Warrior.'

Thoroughly demoralised, Gil stole away into the darkness around the camp to report back to Alfgar.

The first question that Alfgar asked was, 'Who commands?'

Gil answered, 'Earl Harold.'

'Surely not, you are mistaken.'

'I saw him with my own eyes. Believe me, he is miraculously restored and carries a blue standard with a cross of gold.'

'The standard of the shrine at Waltham Holy Cross.'

Gruffudd was exhibiting signs of alarm.

Turning to Alfgar he said, 'You assured me that Harold was a hopeless cripple and would never again rise from his bed.'

Alfgar ignored that complaint and said, 'We must retreat to your stronghold at Leominster.'

Gruffudd sneered, 'So this is the extent of the fabled Saxon courage. You run away from cripples.'

The next morning Harold crossed the Severn at the head of his army, and the rebels fled in a desperate attempt to reach the safety of Leominster. However, they were overtaken before they reached their goal and Harold's men exacted great slaughter, until the survivors fled into the Black Mountains. Harold did not pursue them further as he knew that his men were not accustomed to fighting in a land of deep valleys and high mountains. Instead, he offered generous terms of surrender which the rebels accepted. Being magnanimous in victory is the mark of a wise ruler.

I asked my grandfather why he admired Harold who, when all was said and done, was defeated and slain at the battle of Hastings.

Llywelyn smiled and said, 'The manner of that defeat and death.'

In September 1066, Harold, the newly proclaimed King of Britain, faced two formidable foes: The Viking Harold Hardrada in the north and Duke William of Normandy in the south. Hardrada, accompanied by Tostig, arrived off the north-east coast of England with a war fleet of 300 ships and 12,000 men. After sacking Scarborough and defeating an army raised by the northern earls, the Vikings laid siege to York. This put Harold in a dilemma; did he have the time to march north, drive the Vikings out of his kingdom and then return south to face the anticipated invasion from across the channel? For Harold there was but one answer – he would never sacrifice his northern subjects. Taking the bulk of his army, Harold sped north and, after a succession of forced marches, he reached Tadcaster on 24 September. The following morning, he marched his men through York to make a surprise attack on the Viking camp at Stamford Bridge. The Vikings were camped on the west bank of the river Derwent, where a wooden bridge crossed the river. When Hardrada saw the clouds of dust rise above the road from York and the early morning sun glint on the steel helmets of the advancing English army, he left a few warriors on the west bank to defend the bridge while he deployed his main force on the east bank. The defenders of the bridge fought valiantly, one being conspicuously obdurate, but eventually were slain. This enabled the English to cross over the bridge and hurl themselves upon the Vikings who were deployed behind a shield wall. Inspired by Harold, his archers, foot soldiers and cavalry fell upon the enemy with savage ferocity. The battle, in which Hardrada and Tostig were killed, was long and bloody and ended with an overwhelming victory for Harold.

Speaking to his men, Harold declaimed, 'This Viking, Hardrada, came here to claim England as his. Well he now has six feet of English soil.'

True to his nature, Harold allowed the Vikings who had survived the massacre to sail back home.

Harold was on his way south from York when he received news that William had landed at Pevensey with an invasion force of 300 ships, 2,000 horses and 7,000 fighting men. Not being satisfied with the facilities at Pevensey, he had moved his forces to the port of Hastings, and was now laying waste the surrounding area.

Arriving back in London with an exhausted army, Harold immediately set about mustering new men to bolster his depleted forces. Harold, determined to confront the Normans before they had time to consolidate their defences, left London on 13 October and reached the town of Battle two days later. William, on learning of Harold's advance, marched out of Hastings to attack him. This forced Harold on the defensive and he stationed his men on a ridge running the width of the Downs near the forest of Andredsweald. The choice of this ridge showed Harold's acumen, for although the slope in the front of the ridge was gentle, the sides of the ridge were exceedingly steep, ruling out flanking attacks. The Normans would be forced to make frontal attacks across marshy ground inimical to cavalry and heavily armed fighting men.

Harold's army was made up of 2,000 housecarls and 5,500 poorly equipped men of the fyrd. He arranged his men in a deep phalanx along the length of the ridge with the housecarls deployed on foot to strengthen the line.

Before the battle started, Harold addressed his men, 'Men of England. Fellow Saxons. These Normans and their ilk have come here to destroy your homes and rape your women.

Remember the lesson we taught Hardrada; the only piece of this land an invader will gain is the six foot of earth we bury him in. To each of you I say, remain in your place and defend to the end the spot on which you stand. Do this and victory will be ours.'

William divided his army into three sections: on the right stood the French, the Flemings and the Picards; in the centre the Normans; and on the left the Bretons. William launched repeated attacks against the English shield wall with his lightly armed troops but, when these proved ineffective, he unleashed a full-scale infantry assault with cavalry in support. But, due to the axes of the housecarls and the courage of the fyrd, the English line remained un-breached. At one stage a rumour spread through the Norman ranks that William had been slain. To prevent panic, William removed his helmet and rode amongst his men.

A decisive moment came when the Bretons, wearied by their unavailing assaults on the shield wall, retreated down the slope. A large contingent of the fyrd, sensing victory, left their positions and chased down the hill after the fleeing Bretons, only to have William set his cavalry on them. They were slaughtered in full view of the English on the ridge. The Normans were now able to break the greatly weakened shield wall and scatter the English. Harold took his final stand beside the standards of the Dragon of Wessex and the Fighting Man, with a group of faithful housecarls around him. Wielding their axes, they fought to the death. In the centre of that carnage lay the dead body of Harold, the Golden Warrior.

William denied Harold a Christian burial. Harold Godwinson was unceremoniously buried on the cliffs above Hastings. He had no coffin so they laid him in unhallowed ground wrapped in a royal purple warrior's cloak. There was no priest to guide him on his lonely journey into the unknown.

The soldiers placed on his grave a heavy stone on which were engraved the following words:

A King, Harold, by a Duke's will you rest here,
still guardian of the shore and sea.

After recounting Harold's exploits, my grandfather said, 'Harold and William have been likened to Hector and Achilles. I know that Achilles slayed Hector but I have always thought that Hector was the nobler of the two.'

Llywelyn was a great man and brought Wales under his control – punishing any opposition to his will with ruthless force – but his authority and power depended on the attitude and policies of whoever sat on the English throne. However, by exploiting, with great strategical and tactical skill, the strife between King John and his barons, my grandfather was able to maintain his authority and secure for Wales a golden age that had lasted for twenty-eight years. He showed that, like Hywel Dda, you did not have to die a martyr or become a myth to successfully fight for Welsh independence. The question I asked myself was: would this golden age survive my grandfather's death?

Chapter 2

From internecine strife a new leader is born

IN ENGLAND, UNDER the primogeniture law, all lands and titles are passed on to the eldest son, whereas in Wales, a man's estate is divided among the competing heirs. This situation militates against the emergence of a dominant leader.

My grandfather had three sons: Gruffydd ap Llywelyn, Dafydd ap Llywelyn and Tegwared ap Llywelyn. In an attempt to keep his domain intact, he declared, with the support of the Pope and King Henry III, Dafydd as his sole heir. He then summoned all the putative heirs to the Cistercian abbey at Strata Florida, and made them swear allegiance to Dafydd; thus he hoped to secure a peaceful accession and no dispersal of power.

My father, Gruffydd, had never come to terms with a serious facial disfigurement acquired in his youth when, in a supposed friendly bout of sword play, a large part of his nose was sliced off. This earned him the sobriquet 'Flat Face' and cast doubt on his suitability to be a leader. This was, however, not the main reason why Llywelyn ignored his claim to the succession and made the younger brother Dafydd his heir. Dafydd was the legitimate son by Llywelyn's wife Joan, a daughter of King John, while Gruffydd was a bastard conceived out of wedlock with a woman, Tangwystl.

My brothers and I shared the anguish of our rejected father.

On his death Llywelyn's previous efforts to secure a peaceful transference of power to Dafydd proved in vain and Dafydd had to resort to arms to combat the claims of my father Gruffydd and my brother Owain.

On securing victory, he imprisoned Gruffydd and Owain in Criccieth castle. Two years later he was forced to hand them over as hostages to King Henry III, who incarcerated them in the Tower of London. When news came that Gruffydd had fallen to his death while attempting to escape from his cell at the top of the Tower, with the aid of a makeshift rope, my feelings were ambivalent. I had always regarded my father as a man bludgeoned by circumstances beyond his control, but now I felt a burgeoning admiration for the courage of the man who, in a bid for freedom, was prepared to risk a fall from such a vertiginous height. After my father's death, Henry released Owain in the hope that he would ferment a civil war in Gwynedd, but Owain settled peaceably in Chester.

Dafydd died unexpectedly at Aber in February 1246. For some time he had been suffering from alopecia and the loss of nails from his fingers and toes, but this was not thought to be the cause of his death. The poet Dafydd Benfras wrote an elegy in praise of Dafydd:

He was a man who sprang, great joy of the people,
From the true royal lineage of kings.

Owain and I came to an agreement with Henry and signed the Treaty of Woodstock in which Gwynedd Uwch Conwy was divided between Owain and me, with Henry taking the rest of

Gwynedd. I was far from happy with this arrangement and when, some years later, Henry proposed to give my younger brother Dafydd a part of the greatly reduced Gwynedd, I refused, because I realised that Henry, taking advantage of the customs of Wales, was attempting to fragment the territory. My decision resulted in Owain and Dafydd, my brothers, forming an alliance and taking up arms against me!

I wonder now if it was the Devil himself who conjured up such an evil strife between the sons of Gruffydd ap Llywelyn. Dafydd had only just come of age and had no experience of battle, while, having fought at Owain's side, I had little fear of his prowess as a military leader. I was at Eifionydd when news came that my brothers were approaching at the head of a vast army. Though outnumbered, I had the advantage of being stationed on the brow of Bryn Derwin and knew that a handful of resolute warriors could defend the summit of a mountain against far greater numbers toiling up its slope. Trusting in God we waited unafraid for the coming of this mighty host.

When battle commenced, Owain immediately exhibited his weakness as a commander by repeatedly sending his men to their deaths against a relentless hail of arrows from my archers. The slaughter was so great that Owain's men were forced to clamber over the bodies of their comrades as they attempted to ascend the steep incline. Within an hour the battle was over and Owain and Dafydd were my prisoners.

As I stood on the blood-soaked field with my brothers kneeling at my feet, I declaimed, rather grandiloquently, 'It is the year 1255 and I, Llywelyn ap Gruffydd, am now the undisputed ruler of Gwynedd Uwch Conwy. I vow that I will bring the whole of Gwynedd under my jurisdiction and, before my death, I will be named Prince of Wales – a Wales incorporating the three ancient kingdoms of Gwynedd, Powys and Deheubarth and entirely free from English hegemony.'

Owain looked up and, his mouth twisted in a sneer, said, 'You're already thirty-three, so you'd better get on with it.'

During our joint lordship of Gwynedd Uwch Conway, the only occasion when Owen and I acted in unison was when we petitioned Henry to allow our father's body to be removed from London to Aberconwy and laid to rest with the bodies of his father, Llywelyn, and his brother, Dafydd. In the words of Benfras, they lay shoulder to shoulder like:

Three heroes with sharp blades on helmeted men
Three defenders of their land against traitors.

I had always resented Owain's arrogance, the spurious superiority that an elder brother feels for a younger brother. The younger sees the elder as a natural rival and feels for him an elemental, unfathomably deep hostility which in later life can develop into murderous intent. Think Cain and Abel, Romulus and Remus. Now, I could give that hatred free rein.

Bending down and smiling into his face, I hissed, 'Owain, I'm going to lock you up and throw away the key. You'll rot in a cell until the Lord is merciful and lets you die.'

My feelings for Dafydd were very different. He was young and had been influenced by Owain. Within a year, I released him.

I was tempted to imprison Owain in Criccieth castle, the prison he had shared with my father after being defeated by my uncle Dafydd. Future generations will look back in disbelief and liken our family to a pack of wild dogs trapped in a sack. I saw this as an action inspired by a perverse sense of humour and instead banished him to Dolbadarn castle at the foot of Snowdon, with the instructions that his conditions were to be tolerable – after all he was my brother. When I realised the immensity of the task I had set myself – wrestling the whole of Wales from the grasp of that tenacious monarch Henry – I saw the folly of not enlisting Owain in this great enterprise.

When I entered Owain's cell, I noted the waves of suspicion and alarm that crossed his face.

'Come to gloat at my humiliation and my squalid conditions,' he snarled.

I replied, 'I do not see you chained to the walls; your bed looks comfortable; you are well supplied with quills, paper and ink; you have the appearance of a man who does not lack food and wine. I would say that you have been treated royally, as befits your status.'

In a voice clouded with emotion, Owain said, 'For two years I have been held captive in this accursed place. Day after day, I gaze through the narrow slit in these stone walls and watch the birds mock my captivity with their flight. I curse this pestilential prison with its lifelong lock.'

I answered gently, 'It need not be so. Our family could unite and triumph against the tyrant Henry, if only I could trust you, Owain.'

Owain's face became suffused with the blush of nascent hope and he said, 'You mean you would release me?'

'And make you my second-in-command,' I averred. 'Henry is my enemy not you, my brother.'

At these words, Owain's face expressed his true feelings and he said eagerly, 'Then, together, we will challenge Henry. By the laws of inheritance, the patrimony must be shared between us.'

Ignoring his proffered hand, I said, 'Laws that apply to

petty landlords can have no relevance to the succession of kingdoms. There is but one heir to a throne. You would never be content to serve under me. Your ambition is written on your face. I could never trust you.'

Turning to the jailer, I said curtly, 'Guard him well. He must never leave this cell.'

As I left, Owain cried out, 'Brother! There will be blood.'

CHAPTER 3

Llywelyn ventures forth

Now that I was in sole control of Gwynedd Uwch Conwy, I determined that my first concern would be to consolidate my hold over the territory. Although I was loath to admit it, Owen had been a just and popular ruler and his former subjects were in militant mood. I set up my headquarters at Bangor and, with the help of my council, set about pacifying the troubled parts of my realm. Not, I hasten to point out, by the exercise of force of arms but by persuasion backed by the threat of military action.

My next step was to effect reconciliation with my brother Dafydd. His young face was lined with apprehension as he appeared before me.

Stepping forward, I placed a reassuring arm about his shoulders and said, 'Brother, there is one thing I want you to understand. When Henry espoused you as an heir to Gwynedd, without giving you a part of Gwynedd which lay in his possession, he was attempting to further fragment the Welsh patrimony. This I could not allow. That was the reason I fought the battle at Bryn Derwin, not because of personal hostility to you. Join my council and together we can go forth to restore the principality to its furthermost boundaries and take responsibility for the welfare of our people.'

My council illustrated the extent to which I had succeeded in gaining the support of prominent men throughout the region. Richard, Bishop of Bangor, was one of those fat prelates who prospered whoever was in power. He turned in the direction of the prevailing wind with the alacrity of a well-oiled weathercock. He would make a cautious ally or a dangerous foe.

Iorwerth ap Gwrgunan and Tudor ap Madog were made of very different mettle; supporters of my father, they had, on his death, joined me and had stood at my side on the summit of Bryn Derwin. Iorwerth's ancestral land lay in Perfeddwlad, the region bordering England that was under King Henry's jurisdiction, while Tudor's commute lay in Gwynedd Uwch Conwy.

My mother, Senana, had a brother, Einion ap Caradog, and he was to prove a staunch ally in the conflict to come.

Dafydd Benfras was a poet – it is always wise when you venture forth on uncharted waters to take a poet onboard. A poet can be the eloquent mouthpiece of a ruthless leader and poets are the romancers of history.

My brother Dafydd, having joyfully accepted my offer of rapprochement, was the final member.

It was late afternoon in the summer of 1256 and the council was in session. The sunshine filtered through the stained-glass windows of the cathedral's refectory and illuminated the heavy gold cross that lay on Richard's large belly. As he fingered this insignia of his office, I could sense how happy he was to be back at last in his cathedral after those painful years of enforced exile. His posture of smug contentment I found rather nauseating, and so I turned to Iorwerth and Tudor. They were like two peas in a pod, with their slim figures and neat beards. The only difference being Iorwerth's was black while Tudor's was white, reflecting his greater age.

Einion was very conscious of the fact he was my uncle

and was always giving me the sort of advice he felt my father would have given had he not been dead.

As for Benfras, he would sit silently for most of the time, his keen eyes flitting from speaker to speaker as he followed the ebb and flow of the dialogue. He considered his function as a poet was to record decisions, not influence them.

This day the council had granted a hearing to Maredudd ap Rhys Gryg of Ystrad Tywi. His father had been a staunch ally of my grandfather in his many confrontations with the English, and I was ready to give a sympathetic hearing to any requests he might make.

Maredudd ap Rhys Gryg was accompanied by Maredudd ab Owain, another of the lords of Deheubarth.

When Maredudd ap Rhys Gryg spoke he proved to be fluent and direct, 'Ever since Henry conceded the lordship of Perfeddwlad to his son Edward, the region has been in turmoil.'

Richard stirred uneasily in his chair – the thought that conflict might break out between his former patron Henry and me raised fears that he might again be exiled from his beloved cathedral.

'Henry and Edward have both been abroad and so are not responsible,' he asserted, aggressively.

Maredudd ap Rhys Gryg retorted, 'Edward gave overall stewardship to Geoffrey de Langley, with Gilbert Talbot as his deputy, and ordered them to be ruthless in their suppression of the inhabitants. The people are kept poor by taxes and seizures; their language is spurned and their laws mocked. Gilbert has boasted that he holds the Welsh in the palm of his hand. I come here today to tell you that the people of Perfeddwlad are ready to rise up in defence of their land and the recognition of their law.'

Richard blustered, 'When Edward returns he'll pacify the region.'

Maredudd ab Owain smiled and said, 'Edward has returned. He visited Chester and the Four Cantreds and travelled as far as Diserth and Degannwy. The result? They are more determined then ever to rise against the English and they call upon you, Llywelyn ap Gruffydd, to lead them.'

Iorwerth and Tudor rose to their feet enthused by this call to make a direct attack on the old enemy. Einion, commensurate with his self-esteem, remained seated but nodded his head gravely. The blood drained from Richard's face as his worst fears were realised. Benfras looked ahead to a series of battles that I would expect him to immortalise in his epic poems.

All eyes turned to me. I rose slowly to my feet and drew my sword. Holding it high, I declaimed, 'I will not sheath this sword till there is not a castle in Wales under any other flag but the dragon.'

Now, looking back at that scene, I feel my behaviour bordered on the extravagant. That sword-waving speech would have been better made in front of a rampaging army of thousands, rather than to seven souls in a cathedral refectory.

CHAPTER 4

The battle of Cymerau

I HAVE BEEN considering the nature of war, that activity provoked by man's innate belligerence. There is a beast inside each man and it stirs when you put a sword in his hand. Every part of the earth's surface on which men live has been fought over at sometime or other. War has been the arbiter when other methods of reaching agreement have failed. The outcome is determined by might rather than right. The causes of wars have varied, dictated by place and time. In the past, nomadic tribes fought for good grazing ground; the ancient Greeks died defending their nation; the Romans marched to establish an empire; throughout the ages, religious differences have spawned the bloodiest of battles.

What are the qualities a commander must possess?

The ability to make the correct decisions, the courage to act on those decisions and the strength of will to make his intentions clear to his soldiers. For if the trumpet gives an uncertain sound, who shall prepare himself for the battle?

He must be a master of overall planning and conducting a war or a military campaign, and be capable of manoeuvring forces on the battlefield to achieve a limited objective. Generalship is the science of command. It involves an intimate knowledge of human nature.

A commander should use the lessons of previous wars, paid for in the blood of other men. He has to be a very clear thinker: able to sort out the essentials from the mass of lesser factors which bear on every difficult situation. Once he has grasped the essentials of a problem he must never lose sight of them.

Military problems are in essence simple but the ability to select from the mass of detail those elements which are important is not always easy. The enemy commander is at his best if he is allowed to dictate the progress of the battle. To prevent this one must throw him off balance by an unexpected manoeuvre and thus ensure that he is forced to react to your movements.

A leader must suffer the privations of his soldiers. For I have known what it is to stand in the front rank under a lethal hail of arrows, where the men-at-arms were so tightly packed that the dead stood upright with the living.

Mindful of his great experience and the loyalty he had shown to my father, I made Maredudd ap Rhys Gryg my second in command. Together we mustered a large army consisting mainly of archers and infantry but supported by a troop of light cavalry. Then, on a bright, blustery day in November 1256, we set out to liberate Perfeddwlad. I rode at the head of the column with the standard held firmly in my right hand. The winter sun glinted on the steel caps of the pikemen and the red dragon streamed proudly above.

Victory was won swiftly and involved no major battles. With the whole of Gwynedd under my control, I turned south to Meirionnydd and swept all before me. My domain now stretched from the Dee to the Dyfi. Standing on the banks of the Dyfi, with Maredudd at my side, we gazed across the swiftly flowing river to the land of Deheubarth.

Maredudd spoke passionately, 'Our task is not completed until we defeat those lords of Deheubarth who have given their fealty to the English crown.'

I smiled and said, 'One in particular, I think.'

Maredudd's response was swift, 'Rhys Fychan. He who now rules in Ystrad Tywi, having robbed me of my patrimony.'

I said, forcefully, 'We will send him yelping back to Henry, and restore to you your rightful inheritance.'

Maredudd turned and grasped my hand. I thought an unbreakable bond had been forged between us, but time was to prove me wrong.

Fording the river Dyfi, I drove southwest towards Ystrad Tywi meeting very little resistance. Rhys Fychan fled to England and I was able to restore to my loyal supporters, Maredudd ap Rhys Gryg and Maredudd ab Owain, the lands that Rhys Fychan had stripped from them. I turned east and advanced as far as Welshpool, then south through the lands of Roger Mortimer and captured Builth.

In my pomp I was now in command of almost the whole of Wales. What pleased me most was that the bards now portrayed me as the incarnation of my warrior grandfather, Llywelyn Fawr. At last, Prince Edward was forced to consider me as a serious threat to England's hegemony over Wales and was assembling an army in preparation for a full-scale invasion. On Tuesday, 29 May 1257, I received news that a large English force, supported by a contingent of Welsh soldiers, had entered Carmarthen, having been transported by sea and landed on the west coast. To my very great surprise, I learned that Edward had entrusted command to Stephen Bauzan, Lord of Breigan and Llansanmor – a man who was the antithesis of all that a good commander should be and had the record to prove it.

On the following Thursday the English army left Carmarthen and marched through the Towy valley towards Llandeilo, pillaging and destroying everything in their path.

By nightfall they had reached Llandeilo Fawr where Bauzan decided to make camp. During the night the two wings of my army, commanded by Maredudd ap Rhys Gryg and Maredudd ab Owain, encircled them. In the morning, when the Welsh archers moved into position in the front rank, they were carrying stout poles sharpened at each end. They forced these into the ground, pointing towards the enemy and at an angle that would pierce the chest of a charging horse. Each archer carried a sheaf of twenty-four arrows and before the battle began he would stick these, point down, into the ground at his feet. For two days Bauzan's men were subjected to a merciless, unceasing hail of arrows, and suffered calamitous causalities as the heavy-tipped arrows cut through chain mail as if through linen. When the English heavily armoured cavalry attempted to charge the Welsh lines they were bogged down in the marshy ground and slaughtered. The English now attempted to retreat to Cardigan but suffered more misfortune when their baggage train was captured at Coed Llath by a detachment of my light cavalry. That night there occurred an event that I still find hard to credit – I was sitting in my tent planning what I hoped would be the *coup de grâce* for this insulting army that had dared to invade my kingdom, when two guards entered escorting a prisoner.

'Caught him attempting to enter our lines, sir,' one volunteered.

'He was carrying a white flag,' the other said. 'And claimed to be a lord of Deheubarth.'

I looked closely at the dishevelled figure in front of me and exclaimed, 'As I live and breathe, Rhys Fychan. What brings you to the camp of your sworn enemy?'

Like a gambler making a last desperate throw of the die,

he replied, 'In the past, yes. But I'm looking to the future and I come to offer you friendship and assistance in your heroic campaign against the English.'

I laughed in disbelief and said, 'You are ready to turn against the very people who have come to restore to you your lands in Ystrad Tywi.'

'I look to the future and see you as the undisputed Prince of Wales. I want to be a part of that future, and, if that means swearing an oath of fealty to you as my liege lord, so be it.'

'What worth is any oath of yours? A man who can so easily betray his king.'

'When the Welshmen in Bauzan's army hear of my defection, they will desert in droves. I've burnt my boats and there is no way back for me.'

At first, I was determined to reject his offer out of hand and clamp him in irons, but his words caused me to hesitate. I knew that a pitched battle with Bauzan was inevitable and that the desertion of part of his force would greatly assist my cause. Also, my aim was to rule a Wales in which all the lords would live in harmony, united in their fealty to me. Reconciling Rhys Fychan and Maredudd ap Rhys Gryg would be the first step on that difficult road.

To say that Maredudd responded with fury to my decision to accept Rhys Fechan into the fold, like some biblical lost lamb, would be to understate his reaction, but, with a decisive battle against Bauzan imminent, the resolution of our disagreement had to be postponed.

The following morning, disheartened by the loss of most of their provisions, the English retreated to Cymerau. The time had come to abandon guerrilla tactics and meet the English army head-on in a full-scale battle. I chose a site where the ground was wet and marshy, thus ensuring that the English knights would have difficulty riding over it. When drawing up the order of battle I placed a thin line of men-at-arms in the centre, under my command, with the bulk of my forces on the wings, under the two Maredudds. I deliberately made the centre look vulnerable, hoping Bauzan would concentrate his main attack on my centre. Which he did, proving once again his incompetence. As his cavalry stumbled over the muddy ground, my archers picked them off from the flanks and, when they reached the centre, my men retreated and drew them into the narrow corridor between the two flanks. When horsemen and pikemen were in the trap, I gave the order to close it and the bulk of Bauzan's men were enfolded in a deadly embrace. The slaughter was sickening – many English knights were torn from their mounts and trampled to death in the mud, a fate suffered by Bauzan too.

It is important to realise that, due to the fact that swords and pikes have a restricted range of operation, any close order battle of mass against mass is the sum of individual combats and the Welsh excel in this. As a result, more than 2,000 of Bauzan's men were killed and the rest fled the field, my triumph was complete. Later, disaffected lords spread the calumny that I was not with my army on those fateful days of the campaign. I answer, not only was I present and devised the battle plan, I was the one who led the attack on the supply train at Coed Llath and stopped my men from killing the baggage boys. As every civilised soldier knows, the killing of baggage boys is against the disciplines of war.

Maredudd ap Rhys Gryg had acquitted himself nobly in the battle, but I knew I would have to effect a speedy resolution of our differences. The morning after our triumph, Maredudd, together with a number of his captains, approached my headquarters. I stepped out to greet him.

Ignoring my proffered hand, he cried out, 'Llywelyn, you have wronged me.'

Anxious to calm the situation, I answered, 'Maredudd, let us not dispute in front of the army. Rather, let us retire to my tent where I will listen to your grievances.'

Ordering his men to keep watch, as if he expected some treachery on my part, he followed me into the tent.

Once there he poured forth all the bitterness he felt at what he considered to be my betrayal, 'Llywelyn, as soon as you restored to me my land in Ystrad Tywi, you then returned a goodly portion of it to that traitor Rhys Fychan, a man who has been an enemy of Wales and your family ever since he first took breath. You have given comfort to an enemy at the expense of a loyal friend. Well, consider me a friend no longer.'

I attempted to cool his choler, 'Maredudd, this affair has taught me a harsh lesson. It has shown me how difficult it is to reconcile the aspirations of the lords of Wales with my aim of establishing a nation at peace within itself. It is made more painful by the fact that this harsh truth has been manifested in my relations with you, a friend in whom I placed great trust and love. However, if I am to succeed in establishing such a nation, disaffected men like Rhys Fychan must be brought into our fellowship. It surprises me that you do not appear to realise this.'

'What I cannot accept is that, for political expedience, base traitors are rewarded and honest men are cast down.'

'Then you are not the man I took you for.'

At these words, Maredudd's face turned white with fury and in a voice charged with emotion he said, 'I and my men will leave this very hour.'

He stormed out of the tent before I could attempt to

mitigate the harshness of my words. I knew that he would go to Henry and that I, by my actions and strictures, had turned him into a bitter enemy. I stood there in desolation while in my heart I felt the pain of a lost camaraderie, of a grace that would never come back to me, but in my mind I knew that, for the future of the Welsh nation, I had made the right decision.

CHAPTER 5

The spoils of victory: Llywelyn rules

Now, I REIGNED supreme over Gwynedd, Meirionnydd and Deheubarth. My court bard, Dafydd Benfras, earned his corn by eulogising my victories in what I hoped would be deathless verse. Gratifyingly, the poet and chronicler Matthew Paris praised my achievements and the beneficial changes I had wrought in Wales. He also portrayed Edward as a feckless youth surrounded by unruly scoundrels. The crisis in Wales was of his own making since he had not controlled the brutal and avaricious officials he had put in charge.

He said that the English were a wretched people, but Welshmen were descended from the men of Troy, who had so heroically defended their city. The Welsh were a virtuous people who, under the guidance of God, could triumph over a power more potent than their own.

He concluded with the stirring lines:

Let us stand together for as long as we are undivided, we shall remain invincible.
Wales has found the one prince as the essential instrument of its salvation.

On 18 October 1257, a cloud appeared in the sky and cast a shadow on the sunlit landscape. For that was the day when, in London and before an assembly of the nobles of England, Maredudd ap Rhys Gryg paid homage to King Henry.

Maredudd, when he stormed from my camp, had not gone straight to Henry. This had given me time to attempt reconciliation. I held his son as a hostage and Maredudd, out of fatherly concern, renewed his fealty to me, but, as soon as I released his son, he reneged on his oath. The king's promise to restore to Maredudd all the lands he had forfeited to Rhys Fychan, proved too powerful an inducement.

The loss of such a staunch ally and friend made me determined to make the best possible use of my newly acquired follower, Rhys Fychan. His previous closeness to the royal court enabled him to give me important insights into Henry's character and his relationships with his barons and people.

When questioned about Henry's appearance, Fychan answered, 'Short of stature but of well compacted body and a man of considerable strength. His most noticeable feature is his right eyelid that hangs down so far as to almost obscure the eye and gives the appearance of a perpetually frozen wink.'

'The nature of the man?'

'More of a subject than a king. He knows better how to govern himself than his people. More interested in money than in glory. Why else would he have sold the dukedoms of Normandy and Anjou to the King of France? Yet conscious enough of honour to contend with his barons over their charter of liberty.'

'A religious man?'

'More pious than devout – he takes more pleasure in hearing a mass than a sermon. I would say that his most eminent virtue is his self-restraint, and, after the catastrophic defeat at Cymerau, he is going to have to exercise that continence.'

'Why?'

'The need to launch a major invasion of Wales at a time when he is in serious financial difficulties will cause great strain in the royal council. But launch one he must or lose Wales for ever.'

Fychan was proved correct when, in early August, after several attempts to negotiate a settlement with me, Henry, reluctantly it must be said, invaded Wales. Starting from Chester and using Diserth as a transit encampment, he reached Degannwy in late August 1258. There he waited in vain for reinforcements from England and Ireland, anxiously searching the sky above Snowdon for signs of snow – the harbinger of winter. By 8 September, he felt he could delay no longer and he abandoned his assault on Anglesey and withdrew from Wales, leaving me in possession of almost the whole of Wales. He declared that he would return but his humiliation was complete.

Fychan's observations had given me a useful insight into the man with whom I would eventually have to negotiate a settlement that would determine the future governance of Wales. Before such a meeting took place, my task would be to convert an alliance of lords that was purely military into one that was a permanent political union, and, by the spring of 1258, I had succeeded. All those lords who previously had been my allies now swore homage and fealty to me as their prince. Any lord who broke his oath would suffer excommunication. All that remained was for me to force Henry to sign a formal treaty recognising this change and naming me as Prince of Wales.

My burgeoning status was confirmed when Gruffudd ap Madog, Lord of Powys Fadog, a man who had faithfully served the English crown for seventeen years, now came and,

'

kneeling at my feet, pledged his loyalty to me. I had never made a true friend from among the people around me. My brother, Dafydd, was a fine young man and rode a horse well but there was always the suspicion that he might attempt to usurp me. I was proved right when a few years later he switched sides, only to return to the fold after a brief alliance with Henry. My friendship with Maredudd ap Rhys Gryg had proved transitory and I now counted him among my direst foes.

In Gruffudd ap Madog I found a fellow creature imbibed with the values I held sacred. He had served Henry honourably until he realised that the future salvation of Wales depended on my success. Gruffudd's large sleek body and quiet authoritative voice inspired others to have confidence in his ability. He became my chief advisor and constant companion. We were standing on the top of the massive twin-towered gatehouse of Criccieth castle, built by my grandfather on top of a rocky promontory which juts out into Tremadog Bay and dominates the town of Criccieth. Its construction showed how well my grandfather had seen the strategic benefit resulting from its towering position.

When I expressed satisfaction at my new status, Gruffudd ap Madog frowned and said, 'To be thus is good. But to be safely thus, that is the problem. Do you wish to wear these honours for a day or shall they last and we rejoice in them?

Taken aback, I asked, 'Where lies the danger?'

'The newly crowned King of Scotland is a callow youth, susceptible to coercion from any person more powerful than he. Henry will attempt to force him into an alliance, hell-bent on crushing you.'

'Then I must contact him first and conclude a nonaggression treaty, thus ensuring peace between our two nations.'

'No sire, approach the Scottish lords and make the treaty with them. They will be more likely to honour it than a fickle Alexander.'

'I will dispatch an emissary to Scotland, without delay.'

'Be careful whom you send. These Scottish lairds may dignify themselves with pretty titles like lord or earl, but at heart they are crude clan leaders who would slit your throat with a dirk as soon as pass the time of day with you.'

'Don't worry, I have the very man, Gwion of Bangor.'

My judgement was vindicated when Gwion returned accompanied by Alan of Irvine, the Scottish emissary, who bore an agreement signed by the three most powerful men in Scotland, the earls of Menteith, Buchan and Mar. I received Alan in the great hall of Criccieth castle, seated on a hastily improvised throne and flanked by my brother Dafydd and Gruffudd ap Madog. Behind the throne, I had placed a semi-circle of men-at-arms. First impressions are important and I wanted Alan to report back to his masters the formidable defensive aspect of the castle and the semblance of an ordered court that existed within its stone walls.

Alan stepped up to the throne and kneeling presented me with the agreement of confederacy and friendship in which the lords of Scotland agreed that they would do their best to persuade their young king, Alexander III, not to enter into any agreement with the English king that had the express aim of attacking me. I was amused by the words *do their best*, but was confident that young Alexander would obey his fearsome lairds.

My next task was to reach an understanding with Henry that would finally and irrevocably confirm Wales as an independent principality with me as its prince. I realised that I would have more chance of securing such a treaty at a time when Henry had to contend with an alliance of rebellious barons led by Simon de Montfort, Earl of Leicester, who were exasperated at Henry's maladroit handling of affairs in the English-held Duchy of Gascony. Matters came to a head in the summer of 1258 when, in the parliament at Oxford, Henry was forced to acknowledge the error of his ways and submit to the supremacy of parliament. Believing Henry would be at his weakest, I sent a delegation, headed by Richard, Bishop of Bangor, with the aim of obtaining a lasting peace settlement, only for him to return with a worthless truce. At that time I did not realise the important role Simon de Montfort would play in my life.

CHAPTER 6

The ford at Montgomery

ONE OF THE provisions of the truce was that any disputations would be resolved by an arbitration committee, and a meeting of representatives was called to set up the procedure. On a cold winter's day in December 1258, at Rhyd Chwima, the ford at Montgomery, with the snow swirling about our heads, my brother Dafydd, Gruffudd ap Madog and I sat bestride our restive horses and gazed across the shallow river at the English delegation – Humphrey de Bohun, James Audley and Roger Mortimer.

I tightened my grip on the reins and muttered to Gruffudd, 'Marcher Lords, every one and full of the hubris born of Norman blood.'

In reply, Gruffudd said despairingly, 'And each one of them intent on protecting his territory.'

Many years ago when the Anglo Saxons ruled England, Wales was an independent country divided into a number of little kingdoms ruled by petty princes, but when the Normans invaded and William the Conqueror took the English crown, he placed powerful Norman Lords along the Welsh border. Over time these lords thrust forward from their border bases into Wales, where they built castles. Around these castles they created enclaves and imported citizens to populate them. This area of Norman lordships became known as the March. The Marcher Lords, while nominally owing allegiance to the King of England, were to all intents and purposes independent and were often at war with each other.

For the next two years, after that meeting at the ford, I petitioned Henry in a vain attempt to engage him in meaningful negotiations for a permanent peace, but all I met with was evasion, obfuscation and fruitless visits to Rhyd Chwima. In a mood of mounting frustration, I called a meeting of my council.

Curbing my anger I addressed them rationally, 'You know that my aim has always been to secure a lasting peace, but my endeavours have been met with indifference by Henry. I even offered to sacrifice my cherished bachelorhood and marry one of his homely nieces.'

This aroused a burst of raucous laughter and, raising my hand for silence, I continued, 'Richard here will testify to the tenacity of my efforts as he was the unfortunate purveyor of my unsuccessful entreaties.'

The bishop, stroking the gold cross hanging around his neck, nodded solemnly.

I continued, 'The time has come to consider more forceful means of bringing this king to serious negotiations. When I took over the lordship of Builth from Roger Mortimer, he retreated to within the castle walls and still rules there today with the blessing of Henry. We will lay siege to Builth castle and force Mortimer out.'

Gruffudd ap Madog rose to his feet and said, 'I trust that you will be suitably equipped for siege warfare.'

I had come to trust Gruffudd's judgement and replied, 'The usual weapons, battering rams, siege towers, scaling ladders and projectile-throwing engines.'

Rhys Fychan intervened, brusquely, 'As that list proves, the weapons, tools and techniques of siege craft have not significantly changed since the fall of the Roman Empire, apart from them being slightly more powerful.'

Fychan was no longer the abject fugitive who had changed sides during the battle at Cymerau. He had grown in confidence and become a touch arrogant. His lean body and narrow features gave him the appearance of a vindictive ferret.

I said, dismissively, 'Builth castle was built in Norman times and was a wooden motte and bailey castle. Twenty years ago it was rebuilt in stone. Believe me, it has not the formidable defences of a castle such as Caerffili and should not prove difficult to breach.

It was a bitter winter's morning when my army marched out of Bangor and began the long trek south. As I had assured Gruffudd, my men were equipped with a number of siege engines, prominent among them was a giant trebuchet with its main beam fashioned from a whole tree trunk. We were well provided with the means to hurl projectiles at the enemy – stones, darts, poles, fire or even carrion.

When we came in sight of the castle, we could clearly see the motte, a mound surrounded by a ditch. Surmounting it was a stockade and a keep which was the residence and stronghold of Roger Mortimer, his family and retainers. The bailey was a forecourt protected by another ditch and stockade. The outer entrance to the castle was by a drawbridge, which, of course, Mortimer had raised.

Hostilities began when, to judge the distance, we used our trebuchet to lob a few rotting cattle carcasses into the forecourt. We then scored a number of direct hits on the stockade but made little impression on the massive stones used in its construction. Rhys Fychan's doubts about the effectiveness of our siege equipment appeared to be justified. The thought of having to launch a full-scale infantry attack against an undamaged wall of stone resulted in me having as disturbed a night as Brutus suffered before the battle at Philippi. However, the following morning, my steward, Goronwy, dragged before me an unhappy wretch with his hands tied behind his back.

'My Prince,' he declaimed, 'I caught this villain spying on our camp. He's one of Mortimer's men.'

At this, the captive spoke out angrily, 'I'm Welsh, but like many of my countrymen I was conscripted into Mortimer's army. I've been telling this old fool that a group of us are prepared to lower the drawbridge and so allow your cavalry into the outer courtyard.'

He then pointed to Goronwy and said, 'But it was useless talking to this stubborn octogenarian.'

The steward stepped forward angrily with raised sword, but I intervened, 'I must have time to consider this. Untie his hands and bring him to my tent.'

The outcome? At a prearranged signal, the disaffected in the castle lowered the drawbridge and my cavalry rode full tilt into the bailey, closely followed by the foot soldiers, and encircled the motte. I knew the old adage, never send in the cavalry without infantry support. Mortimer was not present, having been summoned to Westminster, and in his absence, realising the hopelessness of the situation, the seneschal surrendered the castle and was granted safe passage for himself and the garrison. I can still remember the look of pure hatred in his eyes as he handed me his sword. We watched triumphantly as the defeated English crept shamefacedly away, then we started the task of dismantling the castle stone by stone.

That evening as I carried out a tour of inspection of the camp, I heard raised voices coming from the tent shared by Gruffudd and Rhys Fychan. Lifting the flap, I entered to discover the two men engaged in a heated conversation.

Fychan, his cheeks red with anger, said, 'This supposed comrade of mine accuses me of being a tyrant who believes that the end always justifies the means.'

Gruffudd, magisterially replied, 'You condemned yourself out of your own mouth when you said that the preservation of the state might make its prince act in ways that conflict with traditional ethical values.'

'But that doesn't make me a tyrant. The need to preserve the state and the public good could justify many deeds regarded as immoral. What matters in the affairs of a nation are not ethical principles but the outcome for the nation.'

'An embattled tyrant could say that he was torturing his opponents for the common good. I am a moralist who believes that certain ethical principles override all other considerations.'

Fychan appealed to me, 'Prince Llywelyn, does the need to protect the state override ethical precepts?'

This was a question that greatly troubled me and I answered, 'I assume that when you speak of the state you mean an entity separate from the prince. A prince who presented purely consequential justifications for immoral acts would be a very dangerous ruler indeed.'

Fychan looked puzzled while Gruffudd smiled.

I had hoped that the fall of Builth castle would bring Henry back to the negotiating table but it had the opposite effect. An enraged Henry issued a call to arms for a campaign in Wales, only to rescind the order a few days later. He then made clear to me in a letter that he wished to negotiate a new truce for the next two years. This was far from the permanent peace that I craved but on 1 September an agreement was signed that made considerable concessions to the status of Wales and to me as its prince.

In it Henry recognised that I represented the interests of the Welsh people. Henry and I were to retain possession of the territories we held at that time. Trade restrictions between England and Wales were removed. Arbitrators were appointed to deal with any infringements of the truce and were ordered to meet regularly at Rhyd Chwima.

Not all that I had hoped for but a step forward. This episode had shown me that Henry was not in control of his royal council, and this meant that the auguries were good.

CHAPTER 7

Llywelyn humiliates Roger Mortimer and meets Simon de Montfort

D URING THE NEXT two years, the Marcher Lords committed numerous infractions of the truce and repeated visits to Rhyd Chwima proved futile. Appeals to Henry were ignored while he attended to more urgent matters in his own kingdom. In the summer of 1262, I fell dangerously ill and came close to death before recovering. I then heard that Henry had been planning to exploit my death by stirring up dissension between my brother Dafydd, the heir presumptive, and the other Welsh lords. I, therefore, determined to give him something to really think about. Roger Mortimer was the most powerful Marcher Lord and was also a commanding voice at Westminster. His castle at Cefnllys, standing on the rocky ridge that rises above Ieithon in south-east Maeliendd, was a symbol of the powerful Mortimer dynasty. I had already deprived him of his castle at Builth; now I would launch a full-scale assault on Cefnllys castle.

Roger Mortimer was the son of Ralph de Mortimer and Princess Gladys Ddu, the daughter of my grandfather Llywelyn Fawr. This meant that he too was a grandson of Llywelyn. Two grandsons locked in mortal combat. It must be said, we were a very dysfunctional family!

When we arrived outside the walls of Cefnllys castle, the constable, Hywel ap Meurig, a man I had often parlayed with at Rhyd Chwima, rode out with an escort and demanded to know by what right I had broken the king's truce and invaded Mortimer land.

I replied curtly, 'That is a matter between the king and me and is of no concern to a lowly constable such as you.'

Hywel was a man of small stature and compensated for this by having a fiery temper.

He rose up in the saddle and declared, 'I tell you that being constable of this fine castle and being a confidant of the great Lord Mortimer, I am a person of considerable consequence.'

'You are not of the royal blood. You and the garrison must quit the castle. We are resolved to take it.'

A triumphant smile spread across Hywel's engorged face as he answered, 'Lord Mortimer and Humphrey de Bohun, with a large force, are at this very moment marching to our assistance. We will easily resist your siege for the short time it will take for them to arrive.'

With a flourish of his hat, Hywel turned his horse and galloped back into the castle with his escort racing behind him. Before he disappeared from sight he looked back over his shoulder and cried, 'May your royal blood soon stain the sword of Roger Mortimer.'

Back at field headquarters I discussed the situation with my principal officers.

My brother Dafydd spoke first, 'Lay siege immediately and when the castle falls stain your sword with the blood of that impudent scoundrel Hywel ap Meurig.'

Fychan laughed and said, 'Typical course of action from a hot-headed youth. Our siege equipment is next to useless, witness its performance at Builth. In no way can we take the castle before Mortimer arrives and attacks us from the rear. We'll be between a rock and a hard place.'

Before an angry Dafydd could respond, Gruffudd said, 'I agree with Fychan, far better for us to withdraw and when Mortimer enters the castle we advance and form an impenetrable ring around the castle.'

I laid a hand on Dafydd's shoulder and said, 'Brother, I understand your desire for swift retribution but wiser counsel must prevail. We wait until Mortimer and his forces are established within the castle, then surround them. If his army is as large as is rumoured, it will not take long to starve them into submission.'

The next day, my scouts reported that Mortimer and Bohun, riding at the head of a large contingent of archers and pikemen, with banners flying and drums beating, had passed over the drawbridge and under the raised portcullis to be welcomed by the relieved garrison. I then ordered the encirclement of the castle and gave my men instructions to make an ostentatious display of our strength.

Viewing the scene from the ramparts of the castle, Mortimer realised that he had marched into a trap. He would have to suffer the humiliation of negotiating a safe passage for his men from a relative whom he despised as a barbarian and renegade.

Mortimer was a head taller than me and, as he handed me his sword in submission, he stared down haughtily.

I said, with a smile, 'Greetings, cousin. Why not join us in our fight for Welsh independence? I'm sure grandfather would approve.'

Mortimer's lip curled in disgust and he hissed, 'I curse the strain of Welsh blood that corrupts my lineage. You, sir, are a fine specimen of your tribe, a treacherous truce breaker.'

I answered calmly, 'The Marcher Lords are the truce breakers and Henry, despite my protestations, has done nothing to discipline them.'

Mortimer turned his back on me and walked away.

I called after him, 'See that your men lay down their arms before they quit the castle. I thank you for this addition to our stock of weaponry.'

The taking of Cefnllys castle marked the beginning of a continuous offensive in which, with 300 horsemen and 30,000 troops, I spread terror among the Marcher Lords. Then a completely unexpected event in England brought me a powerful new ally, Simon de Montfort.

Simon was an enigmatic figure – born in France he had, on coming of age in 1229, emigrated to England and laid claim to the earldom of Leicester – this claim derived from his father's mother. To everyone's surprise Henry granted him the title and lands, and arranged for his sister, Eleanor, to marry Simon. For a number of years Simon was Henry's right-hand man but then the king turned against Simon and he was forced into exile for two years. He joined a crusade to Jerusalem, where he won great esteem. Returning to England in 1242, he regained Henry's trust but over a period of time he became convinced that Henry was not fit to rule. His dissatisfaction was widely known but news now came that, as the leader of a hard core of rebel barons, he had risen against the king and plunged England into civil war. It was rumoured that this powerful lord was seeking an alliance with me.

I chose the great hall of Criccieth castle for this crucial meeting. I had used the same venue when receiving Alan of Irvine but, whereas on that occasion I had been flanked by my brother Dafydd and Gruffudd ap Madog, and backed by a semi-circle of armed men, I was determined that the only participants in this meeting would be Llywelyn ap Gruffudd and Simon de Montfort. When Simon entered, I saw a tall, slim man with aquiline features and black hair, greying at the temples. He walked towards me with the poise and arrogance of a French aristocrat. Suddenly he came to an abrupt stop and looked around as if expecting some flunky to announce his presence. The fact that I was the only other person in the room seemed to have perplexed him.

I stepped forward and said, 'I felt that a meeting as important as this should be conducted in absolute secrecy, hence the absence of the usual meaningless formalities. We are perfectly capable of introducing ourselves. I am Llywelyn ap Gruffudd, Prince of Wales.'

Simon gave a perfunctory bow and responded, 'Simon de Montfort, Earl of Leicester.'

It was obvious that Simon was ill at ease, so I gestured towards a small table, with two attendant chairs, that stood in a corner of the room.

When we were seated, I opened the conversation, 'I understand that, earlier in your career, you went on a crusade to Jerusalem. Now, there is an enterprise that fascinates me. The splendour of the desert, the courage of the knights, the nobility of the cause with its battle cry, '*Our feet shall stand within thy gates, O Jerusalem.*'

Simon replied, 'Disagreements with the king forced me into exile where I joined Richard, Duke of Cornwell, on his crusade to the Holy Land. We arrived at Acre and found anarchy reigned. The Templars and the Hospitallers were at each others' throats. You speak of the romance of the desert; believe me, it is a barren land swept by ferocious sandstorms and tormented by a relentless sun. As for the courage of the crusading knights, I found them to be a gang of plunderers and rapists. After two years Richard and I returned to England, where I made my peace with Henry.'

I decided to come to the heart of the matter, 'Why have you risen in rebellion against your king? What do you hope to achieve?'

'Why? Because the man is not fit to rule. There was his disastrous invasion of France; his maladroit handling of affairs in Gascony; his failure to honour the undertakings he made to his barons. What do I hope to achieve? A limited monarchy ruling through a parliament that truly represents the people of this country.'

'Does that mean deposing Henry and you becoming king?'

Simon waved a hand in the air and said calmly, 'If it becomes necessary. But allow me to ask what you hope to achieve by this revolt against Henry.'

'An independent Wales united under one prince with its own language, laws and church. All safeguarded by a permanent peace treaty concluded with whoever sits on the English throne. I have had enough of these meaningless truces and these fruitless visits to the ford at Montgomery.'

Simon stood up and, looking firmly into my eyes, said, 'If I am that person on the throne, you will secure that peace treaty. Initially, I do not intend to fight this war openly, but in a series of local skirmishes. The majority of Marcher Lords support Henry; prominent among them is Roger Mortimer. I intend to attack these individually and expect you to join forces with me. Any territory you gain you may keep in perpetuity.'

That night, at a banquet held in honour of our guest, I met Simon de Montfort's daughter Eleanor and was impressed by her beauty and dignified bearing. What did I expect? Her mother was the sister of the King of England and her father was the proudest man in Christendom. I also met Montfort's sons: Amoury, Guy, Henry and Simon. Four fine young men, but the memory I took away from that night was of Eleanor.

During the next few months, our united forces drove Roger Mortimer back towards the English border. Then, in early May, news came that the royal army was marching on London. Simon realised that he must rush to the defence of the capital. The time had come for a full-blooded confrontation between Henry and the rebel forces.

CHAPTER 8

Triumph at Lewes but disaster at Evesham

To supplement Simon's rather depleted force, I provided him with a detachment of soldiers, comprising archers and pikemen. We both were very conscious of the importance of the coming battle, and we embraced knowing that we might never meet again. However, all ended in anti-climax for when Simon reached London he found that Henry's march on London and been a feint and, bypassing Simon, Henry had succeeded in reaching Lewes. He encamped at St Pancras Priory with a force of infantry while his son Edward was stationed at Lewes castle, some 500 yards to the north, with the cavalry. The account of the ensuing battle I learned later from Simon de Montfort himself.

Simon marched in pursuit of Henry and reached Fletching, some eight miles north of Lewes, on 13 May where he set up camp. That night he called a council of war attended by his commanders in which he made clear the daunting odds that they faced.

'Our scouts report that the king has 10,000 men of whom 1,500 are mounted. Against this we have a total of 5,000 soldiers of whom 600 are cavalry. We are outnumbered two to one. My intention is to march out early tomorrow morning and take up a position on the brow of Offham Hill, a mile north-west of the royal army. The advantage of a hill-top position to a numerically inferior force has been well proven in the history of warfare.'

That night the rebel forces marched out and took possession of the summit of Offham Hill, thus holding the higher ground overlooking Lewes. Before the start of hostilities, Simon issued each man with a white cross to be worn as a distinguishing emblem. This would introduce some coherence into the chaos of mass combat. He then split his battle line into four sectors under the command of, respectively, his son Henry, Gilbert de Clare, Nicholas Seagrave and with himself in command of the fourth sector.

Taken by surprise, Henry hurriedly assembled his forces. He took command of the centre with Edward on his right and Richard, Earl of Cornwall, on his left.

Edward led a cavalry charge against Seagrave's Londoners, who broke and fled into Offham village with Edward in hot pursuit, leaving Henry unsupported on his right flank. This forced Henry and Cornwall to launch an attack up Offham Hill. Having toiled up the slope, against an avalanche of armour piercing arrows, they met the full force of Simon's defensive line. Cornwall's men were the first to break and fled down the hill. Henry's men were made of sterner stuff and fought on until Simon brought up his reserves and slowly forced them, step by bloodied step, down the slope and into the town of Lewes.

By the time Edward and his weary horsemen returned from their pursuit of Seagrave's men, the battle was lost and won. He urged his men to continue the fight, but they silently rode off, leaving Edward to ride alone into Lewes in search of his father. Henry had escaped from the mayhem of furious street fighting and had taken refuge in the priory, where Edward found him abandoned, with the town ablaze and all the king's men fled.

When Simon burst into the priory, he found Edward, with raised sword, standing at his father's side.

Henry gently placed his hand on the hilt of Edward's sword and said, 'Lower your bright sword, my son. Our cause is lost.'

To Henry's surprise, Montfort bent his knee and said, 'My gracious majesty.'

Henry responded, 'Fair brother-in-law, you debase yourself. I'd rather that my heart might feel your love than my eyes witness this false courtesy. What you will have I must give, for do we must what force would have us do.'

Simon de Montfort's orders were precise and clear, 'Edward, you will be escorted to Hereford and held hostage there. Your majesty will accompany me to Llywelyn's castle at Cefnllys, still a king but now a puppet to my will.'

'Then I must not say no.'

When Henry arrived at Cefnllys castle, I was surprised to see that, although he was now dressed in the Montfort colours, he still wore the trappings of kingship, even the crown. As Simon and I conducted Henry to the chamber I had prepared for him, I was impressed by his stoic dignity.

On entering the room, he removed the crown from his head and thrust it towards Simon with the words, 'Come, seize the crown. Take this golden crown and compound my grief, while you mount up on high.'

Simon smiled and, gently pushing the crown aside, said, 'No Henry, you take the crown, I'll have none of it. You retain the appearance of majesty but, on your son's life, you do what I command.'

With Henry and Edward, his prisoners, Simon de Montfort

was now the head of a military dictatorship. I have been asked why I did not take the field at Simon's side in that momentous victory, instead of merely providing him with a token force. Well I could say that it was essential that we kept up our campaign in the March, but I would be dissembling. My one aim in life is to establish an independent Wales, governed by a native prince. To achieve this I must reach a negotiated settlement with the English king. If I had taken the field with Simon and Henry had won, my hopes of a successful negotiation would have been destroyed. By only giving Simon a small body of soldiers, the opportunity of still negotiating with Henry would remain open.

I must admit that in the months that followed the battle of Lewes, Simon proved to be a great disappointment. Instead of using our combined forces to drive Mortimer to the English border and out of the March, as I anticipated, we pottered around gaining a few minor victories but not inflicting any really significant defeats on the Marcher Lords. These months also witnessed an alarming erosion of Simon's authority due to the loss of key allies. His vision was of a limited monarchy, ruling through elected councillors and responsible officials. He passionately believed that parliament should be extended to include county knights and burgesses as well as the great nobles, but such radical reform proved anathema to the most powerful barons and they defected to the king's side. The most significant of these turncoats was Gilbert de Clare, Earl of Gloucester, whose first act was to assist Prince Edward escape from his guards at Hereford, thus providing the royal forces with an inspirational warrior capable of leading them to victory against Simon de Montfort.

Prince Edward towered a good head and shoulders above ordinary men, and his strong, lean body made him a formidable opponent in armed combat. His swarthy complexion, close-cropped black hair and eyes that flashed angrily when his passions were aroused, gave him a saturnine aspect that struck fear into the hearts of friends and foes alike. This terrifying fighting machine had but one burning desire, to trample Simon de Montfort's mutilated body into the ground and thus restore to Henry the powers of an absolute monarch. He lost no time in assembling his forces at Worcester and then marched to capture Gloucester.

In late May 1265, I was with Montfort at Pipton near Hay, when this calamitous news reached us. He realised that he would have to join forces with his son Simon who was stationed at Kenilworth. I agreed to strengthen his army by providing him with a large body of Welsh spearmen. I knew that Montfort was a man of great integrity but I feared that he might be tempted to come to some sort of agreement with Edward, especially if it entailed a strengthening of his beloved parliament. I, therefore, resolved to place a spy on his staff and I had the perfect man for the job, Gwion of Bangor – the man who had negotiated so successfully for me with the Scottish lords. Though small of stature, Gwion's body was lean and muscled, and his mind was as sharp as a well-honed blade. When set an assignment, however difficult, he would not rest until the task was accomplished. The reason I chose Gwion was the fact that his loyalty matched his tenacity.

I was filled with foreboding as I watched Simon de Montfort and his son Henry ride out at the head of an army in which Welsh spearmen played all too prominent a part. I knew the force was too small to face the numbers at Edward's command. For his survival, Montfort had to meet up with his son Simon's army before Edward caught up with him. As

Gwion rode past me he raised his sword arm in salute, and I saw, by his troubled face, that he was well aware of the danger that faced Montfort.

It would be two months before Gwion appeared again at my gates. He arrived on horseback, a man broken in body and spirit. We asked him urgently to augment the reports and rumours that had reached us concerning the fate of Simon de Montfort. This he did, one brutal fact after another.

'With Gloucester in royal hands, Montfort tried to take passage over the Severn but his transports were blown out of the water by warships stationed at Gloucester. This forced us to retreat to Hereford and wait for Montfort's son Simon to arrive with reinforcements. But we waited in vain, Edward had attacked young Simon's forces at Kenilworth and inflicted grievous losses upon them, though Simon found refuge in the castle.

'Montfort now led his forces from Hereford in an attempt to cross the Severn at Kempsey and march to relieve Kenilworth and his beleaguered son. By 3 August, we had reached Evesham, but Prince Edward was determined to intercept us before we could reach Kenilworth and after a night march from Worcester his army reached the banks of the Avon at Cleave Priory.'

Gwion stopped and looked hard at me before continuing, 'He then detached a column of cavalry, under the command of your mortal foe Roger Mortimer, to cut off Montfort's escape route over the Bengeworth bridge, while he deployed his own and Gloucester's armies on Green Hill north of Evesham, thus trapping Montfort. The situation was made more desperate by the fact that the royalist forces outnumbered Montfort's army by 10,000 to 6,000. I was at his side when he turned to his son Henry and said, "Lord have mercy on our souls, as our bodies are theirs."

'Now, Montfort was a veteran commander and he knew that the only way to escape was to drive a wedge between Gloucester's and Edward's forces. He therefore deployed his men into a single column with heavily armoured horsemen in the van and Welsh spearmen and English infantry to the rear. He planed to aim this column at the juncture of the two armies facing him on Green Hill.

'At eight o'clock on the morning of 4 August, Simon de Montfort marched his men to the foot of Green Hill. He noticed that the enemy forces were wearing red crosses as a distinguishing mark. He said, with a bitter laugh, "They have not thought of that for themselves, but were taught it by me."

'The instant Montfort launched his column in a desperate assault up the hill, an almighty thunderstorm rent the sky asunder. At one point in the battle it appeared that his gamble might succeed, but then the cavalry wings of the royal army swung in on Montfort's flanks. I am ashamed to say many of the Welsh spearmen broke ranks and fled. The remainder of Montfort's army were soon submerged in an avalanche of attacking royalists led by a rampaging Prince Edward. There, lashed by unrelenting rain, Montfort's men were massacred. His son Henry was one of the first to be killed, then Simon himself was struck off his horse and died fighting on foot.

'There was one comic instance among all the horror; Montfort had brought King Henry onto the battlefield and he, unrecognisable in his armour, went scampering around the field bleating, "Don't kill me – I am Henry of Winchester, your king."

'Eventually, a royalist horseman plucked him from the carnage and carried him to safety.'

Once more, Gwion paused and averted his eyes from the tense faces before him.

He then said, 'It is with revulsion that I reveal the scene that followed. I had been captured and taken to Edward's tent where I was confronted with the sight of King Henry and Prince Edward standing in triumph over the naked body of Simon de Montfort.

'When Edward saw me, he said, "I have spared your life so that you can return to Llywelyn and tell him in graphic detail the fate that awaits anyone who dares to question my father's divine right to rule."

'He drew his sword and methodically cut off Montfort's head, feet and hands. He placed his heel on the severed head and crushed it into the ground. Replacing the bloodied sword in its scabbard, Edward said, "Tell him, negotiate with my father or face the same fate as his friend Simon de Montfort."

'They placed me on a horse and drove me out of the camp, with a cacophony of insults and a constant rain of blows.'

CHAPTER 9

Llywelyn attains his goal

THE BATTLE OF Evesham may have placed Henry back on the throne but dissension still prevailed in the land of England. One faction, led by Roger Mortimer, wanted all those who had supported Simon de Montfort to be deprived of their estates.

The other faction, led by Gilbert de Clare, Earl of Gloucester, wished for reconciliation with the rebel barons and the restoration of their forfeited lands.

I was determined to take advantage of this dissension to obtain a stronger negotiating position when Henry was able to turn his attention to Wales again. In 1265, I captured Hawarden castle and defeated the combined armies of Hamo Lestrange and Maurice FitzGerald, and then I moved on to Brycheiniog and in 1266 routed Roger Mortimer's army.

News came that the Pope, anxious to end the discord in England, had sent Cardinal Ottobuono to mediate between the two factions and ensure that the king's authority be fully restored. Imagine my surprise when Ottobuono arrived on my doorstep demanding an audience. I had Gruffudd ap Madog at my side when the arrogant papal legate, dressed impressively in full ecclesiastical trappings, entered my presence.

Ottobuono, with the words, 'I greet the ruler of a truly Catholic country,' thrust his right hand in my face, evidently expecting me to kiss the large jewelled ring it sported. When I declined, his outrage was comic.

Gruffudd intervened in an attempt to assuage the affronted nuncio, 'Monsignor, what leads you to believe that Wales is a truly Catholic country?

Ottobuono looked startled and said, 'In every hamlet of this land one sees the simple peasants thronging the streets on holy days bearing the images of Jesus and his saints. They fill the churches with lighted candles and revere the relics of the martyrs.'

Gruffudd answered gently, 'But are we not making a mistake when we take these outward signs of reverence as an expression of deep religious beliefs when they are no more than the manifestations of ignorant superstition?'

'What you call ignorant superstition the Church calls faith,' Ottobuono retorted. 'How else can poor uneducated peasants learn to love their God but through blind faith. Can they read the word of God written in the Bible? Can they discourse with scholars? They reach God through the teaching of the Church and their love of wax statues, candles and relics. What do you have against the veneration of relics? Does it not redound to the honour of the saints? Take those things away from them and they will be lost and condemned to everlasting hell.'

Ottobuono then turned to me and said, 'Sire, I bring glad tidings from England. By God's holy will, Gilbert de Clare, Earl of Gloucester, has prevailed and dissension has been banished from the land.'

Gruffudd said, 'No doubt, the fact that Gilbert de Clare had stationed his army menacingly at the gates of parliament played some part in the resolution.'

Ignoring Gruffudd's ironic observation, the cardinal said, 'Now that Henry's absolute power has been restored, he is able to offer you meaningful negotiations that, with God's guidance, will lead to a lasting peace between your two nations.'

The talks were to take place in Shrewsbury between representatives of both sides. Henry, Edward and I would not be present but would have to signify our agreement by signing any treaty that might emerge.

It was at this time that Richard, worn out by his efforts to serve two masters, had resigned from the burdens of his pastorate to be replaced as Bishop of Bangor by Anian.

On 28 August 1267, Bishop Anian, with the other members of my delegation went to Shrewsbury to open the negotiations – a month later, he returned in triumph. King Henry was prepared to grant me the title Prince of Wales and Lord of Snowdon, allow me to retain the land I had conquered and receive the homage of all the lords of Wales, with the exception of Maredudd ap Rhys Gryg, my erstwhile friend turned foe. My brother Dafydd was granted estates within the principality but would have to submit to my jurisdiction. I was now a prince in possession of the three coronets of Gwynedd, Powys and Deheubarth. A king of England had placed his imprimatur on my authority. For all this I was to pay a tribute of 25,000 marks in yearly instalments of 3,000 marks and kneel in homage before King Henry.

I made that obeisance at Rhyd Chwima, the ford at Montgomery. As I knelt there I felt my heart burst with pride. I had surpassed the achievements of my illustrious grandfather Llywelyn Fawr. A king of England had granted me, and those who would come after me, by heredity right, the principality of Wales. Looking up I saw in Henry's weary face relief at the cessation of our twelve years of bitter feuding, but Edward's scowling countenance showed that, as far as he was concerned, this was not the end of the matter. In my moment of supreme exultation, I suffered a sudden, sharp needlepoint of fear – fear of what the future might bring.

Some time later, I realised that, although the treaty had elevated me to a status comparable to that of one of the great lords of England, it defined me as a vassal of the English crown. There, at Rhyd Chwima, we had planted the seeds of further dissension and bloody conflict.

On 7 December 1269, I learnt with great dismay that my faithful confidant Gruffudd ap Madog had died suddenly in his castle at Dinas Brân. The news was brought by his youngest son Gruffudd Fychan, who so impressed me with his bearing and acumen that I promptly gave him his father's place in my court.

CHAPTER 10

The leopard bares its claws

THE INK HAD barely dried on the treaty of Rhyd Chwima when three powerful lords – Gilbert de Clare, Humphrey de Bohun and Roger Mortimer – challenged my authority. Bohun threatened the lordship of Brecon and Mortimer, who was becoming an authoritative voice at the Westminster parliament, spoke strongly against me. The campaign started when Clare entered the lordship of Senghennydd, captured its lord, Gruffudd ap Rhys, and imprisoned him in Kilkenny castle. I appealed to King Henry for arbitration and he submitted the matter to his son Edward and ordered me to attend the prince at Rhyd Chwima. Remembering Edward's boorish behaviour at our last meeting, it was with grave misgivings that I journeyed to the ford. Imagine my relief when Edward proved anxious to establish an understanding with me and ordered that Gruffudd ap Rhys be released and restored to his lordship. I was astonished by this volte-face, but I had been told that Edward was a lion by his pride and a leopard by his inconsistency. I was so pleased by the outcome that I wrote a cordial greeting to Henry expressing approval of Edward's conduct. Henry in reply invited me to London to witness the transfer of the body of Edward the Confessor to its shrine in the great church at Westminster. Henry was devoted to the cult of the Confessor and had named his first son Edward in his honour. I was unable to attend – perhaps I should have made the effort.

This marked the high point of my relationship with the English crown. Unfortunately, in the summer of 1270, Edward went off to the Holy Land to join a new Crusade. His father had taken the Cross but was now too old and infirm to undertake a Crusade; so, on hearing that Antioch had fallen, he persuaded Edward to go in his place. I had always been fascinated by the Crusades. Their history rang with the sound of battle trumpets and drums; glittered with the splendour of magnificently caparisoned horses and noble pageants; was replete with stories of bravery and feats of daring. However, Simon de Montfort had shown me another aspect of the Crusades and made me look through this gaudy façade to the truth behind, where I saw unbridled brutality and rapaciousness, tales of cowardice and treacherous intrigue; the slaughter of 50,000 infidels at the fall of Jerusalem. The Crusades were no place for a Welsh prince.

Edward was a methodical man and he planned his campaign with diligent care. Many English nobles promised to join him but, when the time came, most made their excuses and slunk shamefaced away. When Edward and his wife, Eleanor of Castle, set out, he was accompanied by a force of merely 1,000 men, supplemented by a small contingent of Bretons. He had intended to join up with King Louis at Tunis but when he got there he found Louis dead and the French troops embarking for home. He spent the winter in Sicily with King Charles and then, in early spring, set sail for Acre where he made landfall on 9 May 1271. He was horrified at the corruption and confusion that reigned in the Crusader ranks and the realisation that his force was too small for anything more than engage in minor skirmishes.

News reached England that, on 16 June 1272, an assassin had entered Edward's tent and stabbed him with a poisoned dagger. His life was saved when his devoted wife Eleanor sucked the poison from the open wound. The truth when it emerged was more prosaic – the poison had been removed by a group of surgeons who had ordered that the wailing Eleanor be taken from the tent as she was distracting them. One of them is reported to have said that it was better that she should be in tears outside the tent than all England weep. It was while Edward was recuperating that he learned that his father was dying. Acutely aware that he was wasting his time in the Holy Land, he embarked from Acre on 22 September 1272 and, after calling in on Sicily and quelling a rebellion in Gascony, he finally arrived back in England in August 1274 to find that he was King Edward I of England.

Edward was in a bad mood; his Crusade had ended in failure and had cost him 150,000 marks, forcing him to borrow 34,500 marks, from an Italian bank. His wife, who had always supported her husband's military ambitions, had a translation made of the Roman manual on the art of war by Vegetius and, after having it bound sumptuously, presented it to him. I am sure that he found it an inadequate compensation for his travails.

Edward's coronation was a magnificent occasion, though some might have thought it extravagant and ostentatious. I, as a vassal of the king, was invited, or rather ordered, to attend the ceremony at Westminster, a summons I chose to ignore. The King of Scotland, Alexander, attended and wrote to me, vividly describing the event.

The two halls at Westminster had been redecorated and, as I entered my eyes were dazzled by such beauty and my soul was replete with pleasure.

At the banquet after the ceremony the food was lavish; swan, peacock and boar were carried triumphantly through the brightly lit hall up to the high table, while beef, mutton, pork and poultry were consumed in great quantities by the less exalted guests. The citizens of London celebrated in the streets as red and white wine flowed from the public drinking fountain in Cheapside. The climax to the festivities came when 500 horses were released to be claimed by any who managed to capture them. What worries me is where the money will have to come from. The man is heavily in debt.

By far the most chilling event was when Edward rose to his feet, lifted his crown high in the air and declared, 'I will not put this crown back on my head until I have recovered all the crown lands given away by my father.'

The next day I was granted a private audience with the new king. After dourly accepting my protestations of loyalty, Edward proclaimed, 'It is time this land felt the grip of firm governance. My enfeebled father was too gentle in his dealings with rebels like Simon de Montfort and Llywelyn. If Llywelyn disturbs the peace settlement in the March he will answer to me.' Edward paused, smiled viciously and added, 'He would do well to remember the fate of his friend Montfort.'

Edward then adopted a businesslike manner, 'To assist in my task of detecting encroachments on royal rights, I am setting up an inquiry into local administration throughout the land. The activities of all local officials from sheriffs to castle constables will be scrutinised. When it has been completed, it will rival the Domesday Book in size and rigour.'

I was surprised by Edward's aggressive manner and decided to change the topic, 'Sire, It has always puzzled me with regard to the Crusades how you crusaders reconcile all that murder with the Christian commandment "Thou must not kill".'

Edward answered, 'It has always been accepted that a Christian can kill in defence of his faith. The early Crusades were *altruistic in nature. Peter the Hermit, a monk of unprepossessing appearance – his face ugly, his clothes filthy – went all over Europe preaching the right of Christians to visit the Holy Land. He recruited a vast army consisting mainly of poor peasants and formed the People's Crusade. It was miraculous.'*

'Not all that miraculous,' I responded. 'Life for a peasant was grim and insecure. Peter offered the opportunity for loot and heavenly indulgence. It all ended in disaster at Civetot in the loss of many thousands of lives and taught that faith alone, without discipline, would not open the road to Jerusalem.'

Edward answered dryly, 'You seem very well informed on the history of the Crusades. Perhaps you ought to join one.'

I retorted, 'Perhaps not, considering the unsuccessful conclusion of your expedition.'

Edward laughed and said, 'The crusade was not a complete failure. I made a number of firm and lasting friendships with a group of distinguished lords who will serve me loyally in any future war I might have with a certain rebellious Welsh prince.'

The audience was at an end.

I felt I must warn you that Edward wishes you nothing but harm.

Gruffudd Fychan and I read the missive with dismay etched on our faces.

'Alexander is an impressionable novice,' Gruffudd ventured. 'He might be exaggerating Edward's hostility. Is this the Edward who negotiated so affably with you at Montgomery?'

'No,' I answered. 'This is the Edward who so vilely mutilated Simon's body at Tewkesbury.'

'Mathew Paris is spreading a story that Edward, to satisfy his perverted nature, once had an innocent youth tortured to death. The man is a monster. This does not bode well for the future.'

'If I were a magician and looked into my great crystal sphere, all I could see would be a swirling atrocity of blood and ashes.'

CHAPTER 11

Llywelyn sows the seeds of defiance and reaps a bitter harvest

Conformation of my fears arrived a few days later – an order to attend the king at Shrewsbury on 22 November. Realising the significance of this development, I called a meeting of my council. On entering the chamber I saw my brother, Dafydd, lurking sullenly in a corner. My mind slipped back to that bleak, wintry day last February. Dafydd's behaviour had been puzzling – throughout the day he had been hovering near me, never taking his eyes off me and, as night came on, his attention became even more intense. The weather deteriorated, and he kept looking out on a landscape that was rapidly disappearing under a thickening blanket of snow. I advised him to return to his apartment while he could still see his way. He promptly wished me a curt goodnight and left. A week later I discovered the reason for his strange behaviour. That treacherous magnate Gruffudd ap Gwenwynwyn and his eldest son Owain had plotted with my brother to murder me on that day in February but the blizzard had prevented Owain and his armed assassins from reaching my camp. The conspirators were tried by a jury of their peers who ruled that Gruffudd ap Gwenwynwyn should forfeit most of his land, while my brother was handed over to me for punishment. Hoping to achieve reconciliation, I pardoned him and kept him on my council. Gruffudd and Owain fled to England seeking Edward's protection.

After informing the council of Edward's demand that I meet him at Shrewsbury, I said, 'I know the reasons for this summons and its intemperate tone. He will expect me to pay him homage as his loyal vassal; he will demand that I start again paying the annual tribute I owe the English crown, and he will order me to desist from hostile acts against Clare, Bohun and Mortimer in the March.'

My brother Dafydd responded first, 'He has a right to demand those three things. You agreed them when you paid homage to King Henry at Rhyd Chwima. Prove that a Welshman can keep his word.'

I smiled ruefully and said, 'My brother, Dafydd, siding with the English again. There are times when I wonder where his loyalty lies.'

This was greeted with suppressed laughter.

Dafydd blushed angrily and retorted, 'On the side of those who honour their word and pay their bills.'

'Some might think that not paying the tribute is an act of defiance but, in all honesty, I do not have the resources. Have you noticed the failure of the harvests these last two years?'

After a heated debate the meeting broke up with no decision being taken. Two days later a letter arrived from Edward postponing the meeting because he had developed an abscess on the wound he had suffered at Acre.

It was at that time that Gruffudd Fychan brought me a copy of a heraldic device that showed Edward as a crowned king, sceptre in hand, seated on his throne. Standing at his right hand was Alexander III and on his left myself.

Gruffudd said, 'If this is meant to symbolise the

governance of this island, it implies that you and Alexander are of equal importance.'

I answered curtly, 'Nonsense, that would mean that the principality of Wales has the same status as the kingdom of Scotland. An assumption that is palpably false. Alexander had an unchallenged succession to an unbroken tradition of kingship. Compare that to my tortuous path to power. The second son of a prince to whom the inheritance had been denied, my lot has been one of unrelenting endeavour. The time has come to redress this imbalance.'

Gruffudd Fychan said, with a laugh, 'Align yourself with a royal line by marriage.'

I thought immediately of Eleanor, Simon de Montfort's daughter; her mother was a sister of Henry III, which made her a first cousin of King Edward. I remembered a young girl of striking appearance with shining black hair and a neck as white and elegant as that of a swan. I calculated that she would now be 23 years old. She seemed ideal in every way and there was the added advantage that Edward would be enraged by the marriage.

On hearing of the death and hideous mutilation of her father, Eleanor, with her mother Countess Eleanor, had fled to France and found sanctuary in the Dominican nunnery at Montargis, where her brothers Simon, Guy and Amaury, soon followed her. In 1271, in an attempt to bring the Montfort family into his peace, Edward sent his cousin, Henry of Almain to negotiate with the brothers. This resulted in Guy and Simon murdering Henry in the precincts of the church of San Silvestre. From that time on, Edward kept a wary eye on the activities at Montargis.

The year 1275 did not start well. My brother Dafydd turned traitor again and sought Edward's protection. No doubt there will be in the future brothers as false as Dafydd, but his repeated defections left me feeling very vulnerable. The strength of a monarch depends on a line of succession. He must establish a royal line, therefore I needed a son, without whom the future of the principality would be imperilled. The time had come to contact Eleanor and make her a proposal of marriage. I would be brutally honest and admit that this was no love match but a political action necessary to consolidate my position as Prince of Wales. I sat alone in my study and composed a letter that I hoped would prove to be the most significant missive of my life.

To Lady Eleanor de Montfort

From Llywelyn ap Gruffudd, Prince of Wales and Lord of Snowdon

I trust that the bearer of this letter finds you in good health and secure in your sanctuary at Montargis.

My brother, Dafydd, has proved the renegade once again, leaving me feeling vulnerable and exposed. I now realise that in order to secure my sovereignty I must establish a royal line. Your illustrious father and I often spoke of uniting our two families through marriage. The time has come for the red dragon of Wales and the white lion of Montfort to stand side by side.

My lady Eleanor, I offer you my hand in marriage and with it my steadfast fidelity and my princedom.

Eleanor's response was swift and unequivocal:

Here at Montargis, where, each in a narrow grave, the forbears of my family sleep, I feel secure but I would hazard all to cross the channel and become your bride.

You can take me as your wife 'per verba presenti' before I leave the safety of Montargis.

Earlier in the year, Edward had summoned me to pay homage to him at Chester. I had ignored this demand and had taken great pleasure in picturing him waiting in vain for me to turn up and swear my loyalty. There was no turning back now; such an act of defiance must be followed by a deed of comparable import. Eleanor and I were married by proxy in the church at Montargis and, on a cold and blustery day in late December, Eleanor, accompanied by her brother Amaury, set sail for Wales. Hidden in the hold, side by side, lay the banners of Wales and the Montfort family. After that news we heard nothing apart from a rumour of a naval action off the Isles of Scilly, until I received a message from Eleanor.

Dearest Prince and husband

With the aid of a good friend, I have managed to smuggle this message out of Windsor Castle, where I have been incarcerated for the past month.

As you know, late last month I embarked on a voyage over the sea that separates us. Amaury accompanied me and as we stood on the deck, I felt a thousand hearts beat within me at the thought that we would soon be together. A boisterous wind filled our sails and the ship danced on the turbulent waves. When we neared the Isles of Scilly, the captain sighted a frigate fast approaching us. It soon pulled alongside and armed men, sporting the colours of the English king, boarded our vessel. They searched the ship and destroyed the banners we had concealed below deck. Our vessel was commandeered and sailed to the harbour at Bristol where poor Amaury was clapped in irons. I fear for his life because Edward is convinced that Amaury was involved in that unfortunate affair concerning Henry of Almain. Amaury is a priest and took no part in the murder of that man.

I was transferred from Bristol to London and imprisoned in Windsor Castle, where I languish to this day. I am treated with the curtsy appropriate for one of my rank, but how could an enterprise that started with such hope end in such disaster?

Please Llywelyn, save Amoury and rescue me from this confinement.

This outrage exacerbated the mutual hostility that existed between Edward and me. My principality was being frequently subjected to attacks of ever increasing severity by the king's men and prominent Marcher Lords. It became obvious that he was preparing a full-scale war against the Welsh.

Edward sent Robert Kilwardby, the Archbishop of Canterbury, to deliver a stark ultimatum. Robert was a courteous fellow and he delivered Edward's words with a gentleness that belied their harshness.

'To Llywelyn ap Gruffudd, Vassal of King Edward. You will cease immediately your military activities in the March and travel to Chester, where you will kneel before His Majesty and swear your loyalty to him as your king. Furthermore, you will pay the tribute that you owe to the English throne. Failure to obey these demands will result in the whole might of the king's forces taking arms against the principality of Wales.'

When I responded, Robert listened with great attention and not without sympathy.

'My Lord Archbishop, please convey to his Majesty my well wishes and point out that my activities in the March are in response to the continual attacks made on my territory by my brother Dafydd, Roger Mortimer, Humphrey de Bohun and Gruffudd ap Gwenwynwyn, all I fear, at the king's behest. As a result, I have had to defend a wide front from Montgomery across south Wales to Cardigan. I regard the land of Wales as a sacred trust that has been placed in my hands and I will guard it with my life.'

At that point I paused and then, attempting to control my anger, continued, 'I now come to the most grievous injury he has inflicted on me. Against all the laws of chivalry, he has kidnapped my wife. In the sight of God, I am more sinned against than sinning. If there is ever to be peace between our two nations, he must return Princess Eleanor to her rightful place at my side, and he must call off his dogs of war.'

Robert laid a hand on my shoulder and said, 'His Majesty believes that you and Eleanor are not married and that he prevented the marriage by capturing her before she reached you. In his eyes, he has kidnapped your betrothed and not your wife.'

'Then disabuse him my Lord Archbishop. Eleanor and I were married *per verba presenti* in the church at Montargis.'

'Edward is afraid that, if Eleanor is allowed to join you, her kinsmen outside the realm would make common cause with allies inside the realm and foment rebellion.'

I then raised the plight of Eleanor's brother Amaury, 'My wife is much distressed by the imprisonment of her brother.'

Robert shook his head and said, 'The king is convinced that Amaury was involved in the murder of Henry of Almain.'

'But Amaury is an ordained priest of the Holy Mother Church and is innocent of this charge.'

'He is, as you say, a priest and I might be able to persuade His Majesty to release Amaury into the custody of the bishops. There are precedents for such an action.'

Moved by Robert's conciliatory attitude, I said, 'I would do homage to the king at Oswestry or Montgomery provided two conditions are met – my wife is released and Edward confirms the provisions of the peace treaty made at Montgomery in 1267.'

Robert responded enthusiastically, 'I am sure that His Majesty would give serious consideration to such a proposal.'

I raised a cautionary hand and said, 'I must be granted safe conduct before I venture into enemy territory and to ensure this I require three men be handed over to me as hostages: Dafydd ap Gruffudd, Gruffudd ap Gwenwynwyn and Roger Mortimer.'

Robert's face fell and he said sharply, 'Llywelyn, you know that the king could never sanction that. Through your obstinacy, you could call down upon your benighted country the full array of the king's armed might. You are also in grave danger of the Mother Church excommunicating you and your supporters for your failure to act as a true vassal of the king.'

As I watched Robert Kilwardby and his escort ride away from my fortress in Snowdon, I was confident that he would give Edward an honest and dispassionate account of our meeting. Whether there would be peace or war now depended on Edward's reaction.

CHAPTER 12

Excommunication and humiliation

A S WE WAITED at Llanfaes for the result of the archbishop's mission, I realised that Edward was vacillating because he was reluctant to commit himself to a full-scale war when he had promised to help Alphonso of Castile in his war against the Saracens. I therefore deemed it worthwhile to send Bishop Anian on one last attempt to influence Edward.

The contrast between Anian and his predecessor Richard could not have been more marked. Anian, with his skeletal figure and pale aesthetic face, compared unfavourably with Richard's colossal belly and round cheerful countenance. I instructed Anian to assure Edward that I wanted to be received into the king's peace and friendship but to stress that he must honour the conditions I had laid down. I had an uneasy feeling that Anian was torn between his duties to the church and his loyalty to me.

He returned with the news that on 10 February, following a convocation of clergy at Canterbury, the archbishop had called on the bishops of the province to proceed with the excommunication of me and my supporters, unless we abandoned our obduracy within one month. In an attempt to prevent this catastrophe, Robert Kilwardby sent a delegation to visit me at Llanfaes where I was holding court. I was determined to deny them entry to the castle but I knew that many of my lords, faced with excommunication, wanted me to compromise. I would have to convince them that war was the only way forward. I gazed at the anxious sea of upturned faces and summoned up the will to earn their continued support.

I raised my hand for silence and cried, 'Men of Gwynedd, Meirionnydd and Deheubarth, you are warriors of a newly founded Wales. There can be no bowing the knee to the arrogant English king. He has abducted the wife of your prince. What greater insult could he have inflicted on us? Despite constant appeals, he continues to allow, nay to encourage, the Marcher Lords to attack our frontiers. His commanders – Roger Mortimer at Montgomery, William Beauchamp at Chester and Payn de Chaworth at Carmarthen – are dismembering our principality. Fear not a full-scale war, it will be a better and a braver option than allowing our nation to die of a thousand cuts.'

Lowering my voice, I continued, 'One night, unable to sleep, I rode out onto the bare uplands of the Berwyn Range. Once over the mountain, I took a path through the forest that led to the ruins of the ancient city of Mathrafal. Once there, I dismounted and stood in the moonlight with head bowed. It was at that moment I was flooded with the realisation that this primeval city had housed a people who had been there since the beginning of time – long before the coming of Christ and Caesar. There, on that spot, the soul of the ancient Welsh race lay buried. The time has come to bring it back to life, to exult in the memory of the icons of our proud past: the king who built his palace on a crannog in the middle of a vast lake and traded with exotic nations far in the east, Hywel Dda who formulated our laws, and Llywelyn Fawr, the warrior prince.'

The archbishop's envoys were refused entry and forced to

return to Canterbury. Within days, the archbishop secured the promulgation of excommunication. Throughout the diocese of Bangor, as in the rest of the provinces of Canterbury and York, bells were rung and candles extinguished to proclaim that the Prince of Wales had incurred the censure of the Church of Christ, by his failure to fulfil his solemn duty to his king, and was henceforth cast into the outer darkness. This excommunication was devastating as it absolved my subjects of their allegiance to me. This power of excommunication, when directed against rulers, was the source of the Church's temporal power. Bishop Anian, having performed mass at the church of St Deiniol in Bangor fled, for fear of his life, to the abbey of St Albans where I hope he suffered from a troubled conscience, for his treachery to me.

Edward lost no time in clearing the decks for his war against me. He informed Alphonso of Castile that he would be unable to assist him in his war against the Saracens, as he had a troublesome prince to subdue. He then offered my brothers Dafydd and Rhodri my lands if they joined him in his campaign against me. By August he had assembled at Chester the forces of the Marcher Lords and the feudal host, composed of contingents provided by the lords who held their lands from the king in return for military service. Never before had there been such a great and glittering gathering of the military might of England and never before had Edward commanded so huge an army.

I joked with Gruffudd Fychan, 'I trust Edward has studied well the Roman manual on the art of war by Vegetius that his wife presented him with after his disastrous campaign in the Holy Land.'

Gruffudd shook his head and said, 'Llywelyn, I fear Edward will surprise us with his acumen.'

I wish to draw a veil over the war of attrition that followed. A war marked by no great battles but by the relentless erosion of my military strength and the systematic dismemberment of my principality by superior forces led by determined and resourceful commanders.

Edward had prepared a road along the north Wales coast to facilitate the movement of his vast army that consisted of over 15,000 men. The campaign route went from Chester to Flint and on to the old English stronghold of Degannwy. From there Edward sent troops by sea to Anglesey where they reaped the grain harvest. This deprived me of the ability to feed my men. He advanced swiftly to the banks of the river Conway and was soon encamped at Degannwy. My military strength in the March, Powys, Deheubarth and Gwynedd was deteriorating, causing the defection to Edward of numerous lords and clerics. If I wished to avoid total destruction and save some part of my principality, there was but one course open to me. I sued for peace.

Negotiations were conducted at Aberconwy and agreement was reached on 9 November 1277. Although Edward's position was one of great strength, he was worried about the security of his extended lines of communication and was ready to parley. The terms he imposed were, however, extremely tough. I could retain the title Prince of Wales and Lord of Snowdon but my authority was confined to Gwynedd Uwch Conwy while part of Gwynedd Is Conwy was given to my brother Dafydd. Remaining areas were ceded to the English Crown. Owen ap Gruffudd was released from prison and allowed to settle in Ll n, where I hoped he would fade into obscurity.

My humiliation was complete – stripped of almost all my land and forced to acknowledge Edward as my lord and master. Apart from my now hollow title, I was reduced to the same status I held in 1246. The formalities completed, I was ordered to visit Edward who, in all his pomp, was holding court at Worcester.

I proceeded down a pathway delineated by two lines of smirking English lords. Ahead I saw, seated on his throne, the magnificent figure of Edward, resplendent in the trappings of a monarch. Standing at his side was an elegant young woman clothed in a gown of white satin. Edward rose and held her hand. As they glided towards me, I recognised the long white neck and raven black hair of the child I had once known as Simon de Montfort's daughter.

Smiling, Edward said, 'Here Llywelyn, take your betrothed, with my blessing. Tomorrow, you and your princess will be married in this our cathedral at Worcester.'

My joy was clouded by the thought that this gesture showed that Edward no longer regarded me as a threat.

CHAPTER 13

Oh, for the touch of a vanished hand and the sound of a voice that is still

O N THE FEAST of St Edward, Eleanor and I were married in the cathedral church at Worcester before a congregation consisting of the nobility of England and the sovereigns of England and Scotland. Even King John was present, as his tomb lay in the sanctuary between the shrines of bishops Oswald and Wulstan. The revelries and feasting that followed the ceremony rivalled those at the coronation of Edward, and all at the expense of the king. At the end of the celebrations, in compliance with tradition, small gifts were exchanged between the royal couples. Despite Edward's generosity and good humour, I felt that he was not honouring my nuptials but his victory over me.

The prince and princess of Wales spent their wedding night as guests of the King of England. The irony of the situation was not lost on me. Eleanor appeared at the entrance to her bower with a scarlet cloak thrown carelessly over her nightdress. She exhibited no trace of the embarrassment that might have been expected of a young virgin on her first night. On the contrary, her eyes blazed with excitement and her face broke into a bold grin.

Nonplussed, I stammered, 'Who would have thought – Edward would stand the cost of the whole celebration?'

Eleanor replied with a laugh, 'Llywelyn, you forget that I am Edward's cousin and is it not natural that he would wish to do his duty by so close a relative?'

I said petulantly, 'I presented him with four magnificent hunting dogs. He could have been more generous in his gifts to us. To me a paltry marker for my prayer book and to you a miserable kerchief.'

'Llywelyn, don't be such a bore. These small gifts are the normal courtesies a king bestows upon a faithful prince. The size of the gifts is of no importance. Why are we wasting time on this trivia when it is our wedding night?'

I gathered her up in my arms and carried her into the bower.

The following morning, I woke her with a kiss and said gently, 'My love I promised you a princedom and my steadfast fidelity. The princedom is greatly reduced but my fidelity will remain intact. I have not one illegitimate child in the length and breadth of this island and, for a Welsh prince, that is unique.'

Later that day, Eleanor and I set out on a journey to my court at Llanfaes and an uncertain future.

St Thomas Aquinas reasoned that, since woman had been created from Adam's rib, she was his partner, but only in matters where she was biologically indispensable. Furthermore, in the act of intercourse the man took the active role while she was passive and submissive. In all other matters, another man was a far better partner than she could ever be. I'm afraid I must disagree with Thomas on both counts. In our acts of love, Eleanor was as enthusiastic as I was, while her commitment to our cause, as I struggled with the problems inherent in dealing with a demanding king and rebellious warlords, surpassed that offered by the most loyal of my counsellors.

I was soon involved in vexatious litigation with an old enemy of mine, Gruffudd ap Gwenwynwyn. He had forfeited his lands as a punishment for his part in the conspiracy to assassinate me but during the conflict of 1277 he had repossessed Arwystli and part of Cyfeiliog. Now, by the provisions of the treaty of Aberconwy actions between me, as Prince of Wales, and King Edward should be judged by the law of Hywel Dda if they arose in Wales and by the law of England if they arose in England. Since the territory in dispute lay in Wales, I assumed the case would be judged under the law of Wales. To my dismay, Edward ruled in favour of the law of England, asserting that the case must be judged by the laws and customs used in the time of his predecessors; a ruling he stubbornly refused to change despite my protracted and numerous entreaties. My wife Eleanor wrote to him pleading my case.

To his most puissant majesty King Edward of England

From Eleanor Princess of Wales

Dear cousin,

I write, invoking our joint heritage, to plead that you cease this cruel humiliation of my husband Llywelyn, Prince of Wales. He has honourably abided by all the provisions of the treaty of Montgomery, yet you persist in denying him the law of Wales, in contradiction of the terms of this treaty. All he desires is to live in the king's peace but you appear to be favouring his enemies. This is a path that will lead only to conflict and slaughter.

May God guide your thoughts.

Eleanor wished to include a plea that he release her brother, Amaury, but I persuaded her that this would only detract his attention from my case.

The letter elicited the same reply as all my previous entreaties – 'The case must be judged by the laws and customs used in the time of my predecessors.'

While I was engaged in these time-consuming and fruitless negotiations, the communities in the Perfeddwlad grew increasingly disaffected with the English administration, and the situation deteriorated further when, in December 1281, Reginald de Grey was appointed justice of Chester. I was greatly amused to learn that Dafydd, my turncoat brother, had turned against his patron Edward and was openly talking of rebellion.

In these troubled times, I found solace in the arms of Eleanor. One night as she bent over my recumbent body, her hair fell forward and enclosed my face in a circle of glistening black curls. A small gold crucifix hung from her white neck and swung gently to and fro.

Eleanor whispered, 'Llywelyn, I am with child.'

I held her close and said, 'Eleanor my love, we will found a dynasty of Welsh princes.'

It was at this time that Dafydd visited me at the head of a delegation of enraged magnates from the Perfeddwlad. Aware of his treachery in the past, I agreed to speak only to him.

He strode into my presence with the air of a man with a mission. His hair was now streaked with grey but his eyes still had that cunning, hungry gleam.

My greeting was bitter, 'Dear brother, I assume that your fellow assassin, Gruffydd ap Gwenwynwyn, is outside with the rest of the delegation of malcontents.'

Dafydd replied, 'Brother, I came here in the hope that the plight of the people of Wales, a nation of which you are the prince, would override any differences between us.'

'It is not the plight of the people of Wales that troubles you, but your grievances against your patron, Edward.'

'All the people of north-east Wales who live under this oppressive royal administration are ripe for rebellion and who is more fitting to lead them than you Llywelyn – their prince?'

I shook my head and said, 'My mind goes back to that summer afternoon in 1256, with the sun shining through the windows of the refectory at Bangor cathedral. Maredudd ap Rhys Gryg had come to plead with my council to rise up against King Henry in defence of the persecuted Lords of Deheubarth. I answered that call then but I reject yours now.'

'Why?'

'Eleanor is heavy with child and I will soon have a son of my body. The line of succession will be established and I intend to avoid armed conflict with the English crown, especially at the side of an untrustworthy brother.'

'Then, since you shirk your God-given duty, I will lead the revolt.'

'Then you will be smashed by the power of the English army.'

'Why assume that, Llywelyn? Scotland has always driven the English back from her borders.'

'Because when the English go to war against the Welsh, it is a conflict between two dynasties, but when they go to war against Scotland it is a contest between two nations.'

Dafydd responded with anger, 'But Wales is a nation.'

'How can Wales be a nation when, within its borders, father betrays son, son father, and brother plots the death of brother?'

Dafydd reacted as if I had slapped his face, 'I leave you to revel in the joy that Eleanor has brought you.'

He then turned on his heel and left the room without a backward glance. I was left to carry on my peaceful negotiations with Edward over the lordship of Arwystli.

Then, in the spring of 1282, news came that Dafydd had attacked the well garrisoned castle at Hawarden situated a few miles west of Chester. This was followed by reports of an English reverse at Llandeilo. It appeared that north-east Wales had risen in armed revolt, but despite this I remained firm in my resolve not to join the insurrection.

On 19 June 1282, a date that was to haunt me for the rest of my life, Eleanor went into labour. The confinement was protracted and left Eleanor bruised and exhausted but triumphant as she held in her arms a bloodstained, bawling infant girl. I gently removed the child from her grasp and handed the noisy, little bundle to the midwife.

Grasping Eleanor's hand, I said, 'We will name her Gwenllian as we agreed if the child was a girl.'

Eleanor smiled weakly and nodded her head. She then gave a long, low sigh, her hand slipping gently from my grasp, and life departed her body. I gazed at her pale cheeks and dark eyes. Her great beauty had grown wan as though her youth had fled too soon.

There is a despair that crushes you, another that stifles you, but my despair tore me to pieces from the inside. For me, everything living had ceased to exist. Eleanor was the only thing alive in the whole wide world. It must have been the unbearable pain in my soul that made everything dark.

Until Eleanor enfolded me in her arms, I had measured out my life with battles lost and battles won. How good that we were alone together, with no one to disturb us. I knew that she would never leave me, however old and defeated I became. She lived again in my memory as the world darkened around me.

We bore her body across the Menai Straits to the monastery of the Barefooted Friars at Llanfaes. On the deck of the ship, her coffin lay upon a catafalque draped with the red dragon of Wales and the white lion of the Montfort family, while from the top of the mast streamed the great black flag of mourning. There at Llanfaes, where we had spent the first happy months of our marriage, she was buried with all due Christian rites. As I stood there, with head bowed, I realised, in my agony, that my hopes for the future were as ashes in my mouth and I resolved to join my brother in his reckless rising against Edward.

On being told my decision, Gruffudd Fychan urged caution, 'Beware my friend, unlike five years ago, this time Edward will not hesitate to deliver the final blow that will destroy you. He has proved to be a formidable commander and the forces at his disposal are awesome.'

I answered, 'Despair drives me on. At least this will be one battle where my brother and I will be on the same side. Our family united at last, even if it will be in defeat.'

CHAPTER 14

Llywelyn claims to be a direct descendent of Kamber, son of Brutus

I KNEW THAT Edward had set his mind on the complete subjugation of Wales, and spies soon brought me confirmation of this. His infantry was drawn from many lands and he sent agents to the Basque area to recruit the finest horsemen for his cavalry. By early August 1282, he had assembled at Rhuddlan an army which in quality and size was the most impressive in the recent history of warfare. At the head of this juggernaut he placed Gilbert de Clare. The strategy was simple; after reducing even further the few areas I still controlled, his forces would seize Anglesey and use it to launch an attack on my power base in Snowdonia, thus destroying me completely.

Dafydd's attack on Hawarden had inspired similar revolts in other parts of Wales, with Aberystwyth castle captured and insurrection in Ystrad Tywi. Edward quickly struck back, subjugating Gwynedd Is Conway and Anglesey, his forces made an amphibious crossing of the Menai Straits at Llanfaes. It grieved me that Eleanor's final resting place was now a military encampment for my bitterest foe. It was at this time, with Edward's forces on Anglesey, under the command of Luke de Tany, poised to make a final assault on Snowdonia, that Archbishop Pecham persuaded Edward to let him make a final effort to end the conflict. Pecham travelled from Rhuddlan to my manor house of Aber.

Pecham, like his predecessor at Canterbury, was a courteous fellow but was known to hold that Wales was a wild and rebellious nation that needed correction.

After reminding me that England enjoyed the special protection of the apostolic see, he said passionately, 'By the blood of Christ, come to unity with the people of England and to the king's peace.'

I replied, 'As for England's high standing in the eyes of the Vatican, is the Pope aware of the violation of treaties and the atrocities committed by the English in this realm of Wales? Churches wasted and burned to the ground, women and children slaughtered. I declare my readiness to come to the king's peace provided the king pledges to come to a real and proper peace with me. There is no need for the king to wage war against the Welsh people for they are ready to serve him if their rights and laws are guaranteed.'

The archbishop sighed and said reluctantly, 'All I can offer you is your life and a large estate in England. As for your brother Dafydd, his life is spared provided he goes on a long crusade.'

My answer was unequivocal, 'I will not abandon the people whom my ancestors have protected since the days of Kamber, son of Brutus.'

Pecham looked puzzled and said, 'Kamber? But isn't he a character conceived by the fertile imagination of Geoffrey of Monmouth? He is a figure of myth not history. I am not well acquainted with the tale, but you surely do not believe it to be true?

I laughed and said, 'A ruler would indeed be foolish who

neglected to make use of a device that inflamed the patriotism of his people. Let me reacquaint you with the legend. At the end of the Trojan war, Aeneas who had been second in command after Hector, fled the stricken city with his young son Ascanius in his arms, and came by boat to the kingdom of Italy. There they prospered and in time Ascanius became king and fathered a son, Silvus, who in turn fathered a son called Brutus. It was prophesised that Brutus would cause the deaths of his father and mother.'

Pecham interjected, 'Do I detect Oedipus here?'

'His mother died giving birth to him and, ten years later, he accidentally shot his father with an arrow during a hunting expedition. He, with a band of fellow Trojans, was exiled and, after a series of adventures worthy of Odysseus, he landed on this island and named it Britain. He had three sons and on his death they divided the land into three kingdoms that are now known as England, Wales and Scotland. Locrinus, the first born, inherited England; Kamber, the second son was given Wales while Albanactus, the youngest received Scotland. That is why the first ruler of Wales was a descendent of a Trojan aristocrat.'

Pecham smiled politely and said, 'A charming enough story but not a true one I fear.'

I answered, 'What matters to me is that my people believe it.'

The following morning, Pecham mounted his horse and bending down in the saddle said to me, 'I fear, Llewelyn, Edward is determined to destroy you and there is nothing, apart from unconditional surrender on your part, that will dissuade him.'

I answered, 'Better to die on the battlefield with sword in hand than betray my people.'

As Pecham rode away, a harsh wind, the harbinger of the coming winter, sent his cloak billowing out behind him. It was time for me to keep an appointment with Luke de Tany on a beachhead in Snowdonia.

CHAPTER 15

Edward suffers a reverse

E DWARD'S PREPARATIONS FOR his assault on Snowdonia had been meticulous. He intended to launch his attack from Anglesey and to accomplish this he needed a boat-bridge. He had forty pontoons built and had them linked together to form a deck across which infantry and cavalry could safely advance to the mainland. Luke de Tany waited impatiently for the order to commence hostilities. It came on 6 November, the day after Pecham reported back to Edward.

Dafydd and I had taken up a position on the hills above a beach situated at the narrowest part of the straits. Having poor perjured Dafydd as a companion in arms was not as difficult as I had imagined. We both felt proud to be brothers united in a desperate effort to establish the autonomy of our nation. I sensed that Llywelyn Fawr was smiling down upon us – his family at last unified in defence of his beloved Wales. Early on the morning of 7 November, Dafydd and I looked down at the beach below and saw that Tany had been busy during the night. Surreptitiously he had floated an extensive boat-bridge across the straits and anchored it at each end. It was obvious that an attack was imminent.

Dafydd spoke urgently, 'We must detach the bridge at our end before his men have time to cross. We must act swiftly or all will be lost.'

I placed a restraining hand on his shoulder and pointed to a figure in a black cloak.

I said in a whisper, 'That is Morgan, the Welsh thrall. Watch his antics.'

First, Morgan arranged a circle of white stones around him; he then killed a black cock and smeared the stones with the blood. He took off his cloak and held it high above his head so that the wind blew it like a sail. He chanted spells in Welsh and uttered Merlin's name and made passes with his cloak.

I smiled at Dafydd and said, 'No! We will leave the bridge as it is. It will serve our purpose more to let them gain access to our shore. The beachhead is small and confined; once packed in there, they will make an excellent target for our archers. Also, I notice that, due to Morgan's magical rites, the waters in the straits are becoming turbulent and in time they will destroy the bridge and Tany's men will be trapped. Come, we must rouse our men. There is much killing to do this day.'

We did not have to wait long. With a blare of trumpets and a roll of drums, Tany started his invasion of Snowdonia. The infantry marched and the horses pranced across the makeshift bridge; before them was borne the pennant of Saint George and each man wore an armband bearing a cross. It was a stirring sight but one that would soon turn into a bloody shambles. I waited until the narrow beachhead was crowded with jostling men and riders trying to control their restless horses, then I raised my arm and ordered the archers to fire into the seething cauldron below. The result was immediate and devastating, for with such a trapped target every arrow shot found a victim. The foot soldiers scrambled up the steep slope only to be cut down when they reached the summit, while the horsemen cursed as their horses floundered among the sand dunes at the foot of the cliff. The rising wind had whipped up the swift flowing currents of the straits and the resulting turbulence was destroying the bridge.

The time had come to bring down the curtain on Edward's ill-fated attempt to conquer Snowdonia; I ordered my men to attack. Hurling imprecations, they sped down from the high mountains in great numbers and attacked the enemy with atavistic fury. Terrified, Tany's men turned and fled into the now raging waters of the Menai Straits, but heavily laden with arms they instantly drowned. Many noble knights lost their lives that day, including Luke de Tany. Beyond doubt, it was a devastating reverse for Edward and I waited with interest but increasing apprehension to see what his reaction would be. Imagine my surprise when, instead of another assault on Snowdonia, he sent John of Wales to negotiate an end to the conflict. John was a celebrated Franciscan friar and writer, who had a great admiration for the ancient world.

He began a little nervously, 'His Majesty had intended to send Archbishop Pecham but he is indisposed and unable to travel. Hence I stand before you, an inadequate surrogate.'

I responded robustly, 'Nonsense. You were chosen because you were born in Wales and Edward thought you might get a more sympathetic hearing.'

'I regret that the proposals I bring offer nothing new in substance. If you, Llywelyn, agree to an unconditional surrender, His Majesty is prepared to grant you a large estate in England and the title of Earl.'

My reply was robust, 'An earldom in England? Why should I wish to live in a land where I was unaccustomed to the language and the customs?

'I would submit to the king's grace if I was able to do so with honour, but I find his proposals unacceptable, since they spell the destruction of my people rather than their honour and security. I am the lineal descendent of Kamber, one of the three sons of Brutus, the Trojan. The sons who, after the death of their father, shared the kingdom of Britain between them.'

At the mention of ancient Britain, John's eyes lit up and he listened to me with greater interest.

I continued, 'This history deepens my sense of the responsibility I now carry. It is my duty to ensure that this inheritance remains unimpaired. Tell Edward that I will never yield Snowdonia where there is an unwavering trust between me and the people – as he has recently learnt to his cost.'

Dafydd now intervened, 'My brother says no. What do you offer me?'

A look of contempt spread across John's face and he said, 'Your life and a long crusade to the Holy Land.'

'Nothing new there then. Therefore my answer is also no and tell Edward that when I go to the Holy Land I will do so of my own free will and it will be for God and not for him.'

For the first time in my life, I felt proud of my brother. At last my brother and I were united and together we would form the head and shield of the Welsh nation.

News came from the March that my old foe Roger Mortimer had died, leaving two sons Edmund and Roger. Neither of them was too pleased when Edward put Roger Lestrange in charge of the royal forces in the March. A little later I received a confidential message from Edmund, the contents of which gave me considerable cause for thought. I needed to talk to Dafydd and my trusted confidant, Gruffudd Fychan.

'We know that Edward will make a second attempt to establish a bridgehead on Snowdonia, but he will couple this with an attack from another direction. It is therefore imperative that I recruit more soldiers and create a diversion by attacking the March.'

Dafydd asked, 'But how can you do that when you are needed here to defend Snowdonia?'

'God has provided the means. I have a message from Edmund in which he states that he and his brother Roger are having difficulty in repressing outbreaks of rebellion in the March and he invites me to come to Builth where they will swear loyalty to me.'

Gruffudd frowned and said, 'This could well be a trap. Why would the sons of your bitterest enemy now wish to join you in your conflict with the king?'

'There is great turmoil in the March and such circumstances make for strange bedfellows.'

A deeply worried Dafydd intervened, 'But who will defend Snowdonia when you are gone?'

I slapped him on the shoulder and said, 'You, brother. If we just stay here and do nothing we will be overwhelmed. I will take half of our host and march to Builth, gathering more soldiers on the way. By the time I reach Builth I will be at the head of a mighty army and well capable of seeing off any trap, if indeed there should be one. Once I start my incursions into the March, Edward will have to withdraw troops from the Snowdonia campaign and send them against me. I have every confidence, Dafydd, in your ability to defend our position here.'

I then added with a laugh, 'Remember to use the services of Morgan the thrall.'

I had put on a brave face but inwardly I knew too well the desperate nature of our situation. I was venturing into a region dominated by Edmund and Roger Mortimer, Gruffydd ap Gwenwynwyn and Roger Lestrange – magnates who had every reason to hate me. I was relying on augmenting my force as I marched to the meeting place, something that was by no means certain. But I had no choice since, if I stayed on Snowdonia and allowed Edward to attack us from all directions, we would be annihilated and our cause lost for ever.

On the day of my departure, Dafydd and I stood before the massed ranks of our armies.

I embraced him and said, 'My brother, remember that Snowdonia, though a barren land, is an intrinsic part of our inheritance. Defend it with your life.'

I mounted my horse and rode off at the head of a body of men consisting of cavalry, archers and pikemen. On parting from my brother, I was filled with the same foreboding as when I had watched Simon de Montfort ride out to meet a hideous death. There then rose before me the face of Eleanor when her fingers slipped from my grasp and she died. I now knew why I had risked all to join my brother's revolt against Edward.

CHAPTER 16

The final solution

GRUFFUDD FYCHAN rode beside me as we ventured into the March.

Tightening the reins, I said hoarsely, 'I feel a great sense of guilt.'

Surprised, Gruffudd asked abruptly, 'About what?'

'I should have ordered you to stay in Snowdonia and assist my brother Dafydd. He will need all the help he can get. But I, selfishly, wanted you at my side. Edward and the barons of the March see my death as the final solution to the problem of Wales. From the moment when I first set eyes on you, I knew you were of the same mettle as your father, and, by God, I loved that man. If we are riding into a trap, you are the warrior I would choose to stand beside me as I fought for my life.'

'Sire, I would lay down my life to preserve yours.'

'Well, let's hope it doesn't come to that.'

I gave a short laugh and spurred my horse forward.

Whenever we reached the outskirts of a town, I would dismount and, accompanied by a few of my personal bodyguards, I would walk to the market square and converse with the people I found there. They received me cordially enough but the number coming forward to join my force was disappointing. All seemed aware of the awesome army Edward was sending into the field. This meant that the force I was leading to meet the Marcher Lords was considerably less formidable than I had hoped.

On reaching the vicinity of Builth, we crossed the bridge at Orewin and were immediately confronted by the combined forces of Edmund and Roger Mortimer, Gruffydd ap Gwenwynwyn and Roger Lestrange. I had ridden into a trap. It was obvious that the enemy was poised to launch a full-scale attack and I had to muster my forces immediately. I placed my archers on the flanks and my infantry and cavalry in the centre. Each archer carried a sheaf of twenty-four arrows and he stuck these, point down, into the ground at his feet. Tragically, there was not enough time for each archer to deploy the customary sharpened pole. This meant that the cavalry would not be inhibited by the thought of a hidden hedgehog of stakes and so would charge right through the archers. Our flanks were contemptuously swept aside, and then there followed a massive onslaught on our centre by cavalry supported by infantry. There is nothing in the annals of battle more impressive than the beginning of a cavalry charge, the horsemen booting their mounts, large hunter-type horses, to form a line two or three rows deep. The riders sitting high in their saddles, legs straight and thrust forward. Lance under right arm with the left free to manage the reins. The thunder of hoofs as the horsemen, riding knee to knee, spur their horses into a gallop. When a terrified horse crashes into a stationary soldier there is but one outcome. My men fought valiantly but were overwhelmed. Lost sword and broken lance, I struggled to prevent my enemies dragging me from my horse and trampling me to death on the blood soaked ground. Suddenly I was surrounded by Gruffudd Fychan and four housecarls.

Gruffudd shouted above the clamour of battle, 'Sire, the day is lost. Our men flee the field. We will escort you to safety.'

On leaving the scene, I saw that a band of Roger Lestrange's horsemen had noticed our flight and now set off in pursuit.

We entered a wood at Aberedw where Gruffudd spoke boldly, 'Llywelyn, we are hidden for the moment. The battle has been lost but not our cause, provided you live. Therefore I and my men will ride back out of this wood and let them chase us, thus giving you the chance to escape.'

Before I could remonstrate, they wheeled round and rode swiftly out of the wood. The English, being slow-witted, did not notice that I was no longer there and gave pursuit.

The day was shading into dusk when I rode out of the wood and followed a bridle path. Although the sounds of battle – the ring of sword on helm, the neighing of terrified horses and the dismal cries of dying men – had faded into silence, my appearance – shattered shield hanging on a bloodied arm, broken lance lying uselessly across the saddle horn and an empty scabbard flapping against the horse's flank – bore witness to the carnage that had taken place on a battlefield so very near.

My gentle progress was halted when a knight in full armour, mounted on a great black stallion, suddenly appeared and blocked my path. The knight lowered his lance and charged full tilt at me. The point of the lance pierced my breastplate and catapulted me off my horse and onto the ground where I lay with arms extended as if in supplication. Blood trickled from my open mouth and I died with a look of mild surprise on my face.

Epilogue

THE KNIGHT, UNAWARE of the status of his victim, rode off into the gathering gloom. This chance encounter destroyed the hopes of a nation.

Llywelyn's body was discovered by a group of Lestrange's men. They searched his pockets and discovered a number of items including his privy seal.

The leader of the group hacked off Llywelyn's head and placed it in his saddlebag, saying, 'I'm off to Rhuddlan where the king will reward me handsomely for this trophy.'

The others flung the headless body carelessly over the back of one of the horses and followed him.

Edward had the head displayed before the English troops based in Anglesey and it was then dispatched to London were it was placed in a pillory and crowned with a circlet of ivy, as a derisive reference to an old Welsh prophesy that a Welshman would be crowned in London as the king of the whole of Britain. It finally came to rest above the gatehouse at the Tower of London where it remained for many years.

Llywelyn's mutilated body was laid to rest at the Cistercian abbey at Abbeycwmhir on 28 December 1282.

Dafydd, named as Llywelyn's successor, carried on the struggle for several months, but Edward had the boat-bridge repaired and effected a crossing of the Menai Straits at Bangor. This was coordinated with attacks along the Conwy and Ledr valleys. The Welsh will to carry on the struggle was broken and Dafydd became a fugitive, mercilessly hunted down by the English troops. In June 1283, he, together with his family, was captured at Bera Mountain in Snowdonia and brought before Edward, who had him taken to Shrewsbury where, at a special session of Parliament, he was sentenced to death. The method of his execution was vicious and sadistic. Dafydd was dragged through the streets on a hurdle; he was then hanged and, still alive, disembowelled and his entrails burned. Finally, his body was quartered and sent to the four corners of the kingdom while his head was displayed beside the head of Llywelyn above the gatehouse at the Tower of London. Although the sentence was mandatory for the crime of treason, Edward could have mitigated its more barbaric aspects, had he so desired. Determined to exterminate a defeated lineage, Edward hunted down Dafydd's two sons, Llywelyn and Owen, and imprisoned them in Bristol castle. Llywelyn died in 1287 but his brother suffered prolonged imprisonment in a timber cage bound in iron. Dafydd's daughters were sent to the priory at Sixhills.

Knowing that his position was now secure, Edward released Eleanor's brother Amaury and banished him from the kingdom.

Gruffudd Fychan eluded his pursuers and survived the war. He eventually made his peace with Edward and died tranquilly at home in 1289.

Llywelyn's young daughter Gwenllian was taken to the nunnery at Sempringham where she lived in seclusion for the fifty-four years of her life. She was a gentle soul and held in great esteem.

Following his subjugation of Wales, Edward consolidated his victory by building castles at Conwy, Caernarfon, Harlech and Criccieth.

On a windy March night in 1286, Alexander, King of Scotland, fell from his horse and tumbled down a cliff to his death. This started a war between England and Scotland that lasted into the reign of Edward III.

In 1290, Edward's wife, Eleanor of Castile, died and his grief matched that experienced by Llywelyn when his Eleanor died. Edward had two elaborate tombs built, one at Lincoln for her entrails and one at Westminster for her embalmed body.

Edward's prestige on the continent was at its height and, apart from a minor eruption in 1296, which he easily quelled, the Welsh remained acquiescent. This enabled him to engage in war with the French.

On 7 July 1307, on his way to fight the Scots, he succumbed to an illness that had troubled him throughout the previous winter. One rather macabre story is that he asked that his dead body be boiled until clean of flesh; the skeleton should then be taken on every expedition against the Scots. A more rational wish was that his heart be cut out and taken to the Holy Land, and that funds be provided to send one hundred knights on a year-long crusade. Neither wish was carried out; his body was interred at Westminster Abbey in a plain, undecorated tomb.

Llywelyn's life and death confronts us with a puzzling contradiction – he was the only Welsh leader to be officially recognised by the English as Prince of Wales, yet, within a year of his death, Wales lay crushed beneath a brutal English heel.

The poet Gruffudd ab yr Ynad Coch composed an elegy expressing the anguish of the Welsh nation at the death of Llywelyn.

See you not the rush of wind and rain?
See you not the oak trees in turmoil?
See you not that the sea is lashing the shore?
See you not that the truth is portending?

See you not that the sun is hurtling the sky?
See you not that the stars have fallen?
Do you not believe in God, foolish men?
See you not that the world is ending?
Ah, God, that the sea would cover the land!
What is left us that we should linger?
No place of escape from terror's prison,
No place to live: wretched is living!
No counsel, no clasp, not a single path
Open to be saved from fear's sad strife.

Head cut off, no hate so dreadful,
Head cut off, thing better not done,
Head of a soldier, head of praise,
Head of a warlord, dragon's head,
Head of fair Llywelyn: harsh fear strikes the world,
An iron spike through it.
Head of my prince – harsh pain for me –
Head of my soul rendered speechless.
Head that owned honour in nine hundred lands,
Nine hundred feasts were his.
Head of a king, his hand hurled iron,
Head of a king's hawk, forcing a gap.
Head of a kingly wolf out thrusting,
Head of heaven's kings be his haven!

The poets portrayed a leader of honour, engaged in an unequal conflict with an adversary who possessed far more resources than he. They saw him as a prince who could express himself with passion and was profoundly conscious of his dignity and status. He was the warrior prince and his stand at Snowdonia has been likened to that of Leonidas at Thermopylae. He will be remembered for his brave and glorious defence of his country, its laws, its rights and its independence.

It would be in the reign of Henry IV, over a hundred years later, before another Welsh hero raised the banner of revolt against English hegemony. His name was Owain Glyn Dŵr and he is the one man who can claim the title, The Last Prince of Wales.

The legend of Brutus and the island of Albion

*A legend is a traditional narrative that aspires
to be regarded as historical but is unauthenticated.*

AENEAS, THE TROJAN hero, was the son of Anchises and Aphrodite. In his early childhood he was brought up in the mountains but when he was five his father brought him to the city where he completed his education. He grew up to be the bravest of the Trojans after Hector and fought at his side against the invading Greeks, twice engaging Achilles in combat. On both occasions his life was saved by the intervention of the Gods. The first encounter took place on Mount Ida where he was rescued by Zeus' protective hand. They met again in the fighting around the body of Patroclus where Poseidon enveloped Aeneas in a cloud and snatched him to safety. Every assault on the city was driven back by the defenders and the Greeks were forced to resort to trickery. They withdrew their forces and pretended that they had abandoned their attempt to conquer Troy. They left an enormous wooden horse as a gift, which the naive Trojans promptly hauled into the city. That night a group of armed men concealed within the horse emerged and opened the city gates so that the Greek warriors were able to storm in and indulge in pillage and slaughter.

Aeneas escaped through the flames of the stricken city with

his young son Ascanius in his arms. Securing a boat and with a crew of fugitive Trojans, they took to sea and after many adventures they reached Italy, where King Latinus received them with all honour. For a period Aeneas prospered but Turnus, king of the Rutuli, became jealous of the Trojan's advancement and declared war against him. In the ensuing battle Aeneas was victorious and Turnus was slain. Emboldened by this triumph Aeneas seized the kingdom of Italy and married Lavinia, who was the daughter of Latinus. On the death of Aeneas, his son Ascanius was elected king and fathered a son called Silvius. In time he married Lavinia's niece and the union produced a son called Brutus, though there were ugly rumours, swiftly suppressed, that Lavinia was the mother of the child. Before the birth, soothsayers warned that the child would cause the deaths of his parents. They were not wrong; his mother died giving birth to him and, when he reached the age of fifteen, he accidentally shot an arrow through his father's heart while they were out stag hunting. For this patricide he was banished from the kingdom of Italy and, with a band of comrades, he set sail for Greece. On making landfall he discovered a colony of Trojans who were held captive by Pandrasus, king of the Greeks. Realising that these people were of his race and had been brought to Greece as slaves after the fall of Troy, Brutus resolved to free them from this servitude. Among the Greek nobility was a young man called Assaracus who held three castles. His mother was a Trojan and he was deeply troubled by the plight of the captive exiles. When Brutus was elected leader of the Trojans, who numbered 7,000 fighting men, he joined forces with Assaracus. They fortified the castles and occupied the open woodlands and hills with their remaining forces. Brutus then sent a message to Pandrasus:

I Brutus, leader of the Trojans send my greeting to King Pandrasus. My people have withdrawn to the hidden depths of the forests and hills because they can no longer suffer the indignity of being treated in a manner not compatible with their noble ancestry. If this offends you, do not hold it against them but rather praise them, for it is only natural that all those who suffer in captivity should strive to return to their former dignity. Therefore, bestow upon them their lost freedom and give them permission to inhabit the forest glades they now occupy or allow them to leave your kingdom and seek sanctuary in other lands.

Pandrasus was ill pleased with this demand from a subject people and decided to teach them a lesson. He assembled a great army and set off in search of the Trojans. His soldiers marched unconcerned past the castle Sparatinum, unaware that during the previous night Brutus had captured the castle and garrisoned it with 3,000 of his own men. As the Greeks passed by, Brutus made a sally from the castle and caught them completely by surprise. In the mayhem that followed the Greeks were slaughtered and a delighted Brutus rushed to and fro, wielding his bloodied sword.

Antigonus, a brother of Pandrasus, watched in horror this humiliating defeat of the Greeks and determined to do something about it. He gathered together the scattered forces into a formation and with the rallying cry, 'It is better to meet death fighting than die in cowardly flight,' charged straight into the rampaging Trojans. All to no avail; Antigonus and his friend Anacletus were captured and very few of his soldiers escaped death. Victory having been achieved, Brutus garrisoned the castle with 600 soldiers and set off for the forest-groves where the Trojan women and children awaited news of the battle.

Pandrasus, furious at the defeat and the capture of his brother, reassembled his demoralised forces and laid siege to the castle using assault-machines of every description. Standing on the battlements the defenders hurled down missiles and brimstone torches. When the enemy attempted to dig under the walls they were repulsed by Greek fire and boiling water. In time, the defenders, weakened by lack of food and water, sent a message to Brutus asking him to come to their assistance. Brutus knew that he did not have enough men to defeat Pandrasus in a pitched battle and lift the siege, so he needed to devise a subterfuge. He had the captive Anacletus brought before and, holding a dagger to his throat, said, 'My dear friend, unless you agree to do what I am about to tell you, this dagger will end your life and that of your friend Antigonus.'

He then outlined his plan, 'This coming night I intend to attack the Greek camp and slaughter them when they least expect it. To do this I need to distract the sentinels and that is where you come in. You will explain that you have freed Antigonus and hidden him in the woods but because of his heavy chains he can move no further. You will then lead them into the woods where I will be waiting with a band of armed men ready to kill them. This will leave the sleeping camp at our mercy.'

Terrified at the prospect of losing his life and that of his friend, Anacletus played his part to perfection with the result that King Pandrasus was taken prisoner and most of his army slaughtered as they slept. Overjoyed at his victory, Brutus called together his elders and they debated what they should demand of Pandrasus in return for sparing his life. Some thought that they should demand a third of his kingdom and settle in Greece. The majority, however, felt that such a decision would lead to perpetual conflict with the Greeks. They felt that Brutus should demand that Pandrasus grant them permission to emigrate and furnish them with ships, silver, gold and all things that would be useful to them on their journey. In addition they instructed Brutus to ask Pandrasus for the hand in marriage of his eldest daughter, Ignoge. The Greek king was brought in and placed, bound hand and foot, in their midst. He was told that if he did not agree to their demands he would suffer the most painful death imaginable.

He answered in haste, 'Since the Gods are hostile to me, I must obey your commands, although against my will. With regard to my daughter, I take some comfort in the knowledge that I am about to give her to a young man of such great prowess and nobility.'

Pandrasus was released from his chains and, true to his word, he gathered ships from all the shores of Greece and gave them to Brutus together with copious quantities of silver, gold and grain. After the wedding of Brutus and Ignoge, the Trojans sailed away from the land of Pandrasus in 324 Greek vessels, with Brutus leading the way. Standing on the high poop of Brutus' ship, Ignoge wept as her beloved homeland disappeared in the distance.

The Trojans sailed for two days and reached the island of Leogetia, which had been made uninhabitable by constant pirate attacks. Brutus lead a party of 300 armed men in an exploration of the island and found its pastures and woodlands fecund with wild animals but devoid of human beings. They came to a deserted city and found in its centre a temple to Diana with a statue of the goddess standing before the altar. Brutus was aware of the legend that the statue would give answers to any questions put to it. Standing before the altar, with a vessel containing wine and the blood of a sacrificed white hind, he addressed the statue, 'O powerful goddess, tell me which lands you wish us to inhabit. Tell me of a safe dwelling place for my people.'

Four times Brutus proceeded around the altar, each time pouring the wine upon the sacrificial hearth and repeating his plea.

He then lay down on the ground and fell into a profound sleep in which the goddess rose before him and declared, 'Brutus, beyond the setting of the sun, past the realms of Gaul, there lies an island where giants reign supreme. Down the years it will prove to be a home suited to you and your people and for your descendents it will be a second Troy. A race of kings will be born there of your stock, and the whole earth will be subject to them.'

On wakening from this mystic dream, Brutus told his men the answer given by the deity. The men, delighted by the words of the goddess, determined to set sail immediately for this promised land, despite not knowing the direction they should take. After thirty days they reached Africa then they came to the Altars of the Philistines and to Salt-pan Lake and from there they sailed between Russicada and the mountains of Zarec.

Throughout their odyssey they were attacked by pirates and often suffered from lack of food and drink. Landing in Mauretania, they replenished their food stock and then set sail for the Pillars of Hercules where those deep-sea monsters, the Sirens, almost succeeded in sinking their ships. On making land they came across four generations born to exiles from Troy. They were led by a man called Corineus, who was wise in counsel and of great courage. Realising the man's worth, Brutus took him into alliance together with his people. With their numbers greatly increased and their spirits high, the Trojans set sail for Aquitaine. On reaching their destination, they entered the estuary of the Loire and cast anchor intending to explore the region. When Goffar the Pict, who ruled Aquitaine, learned that a mighty fleet of ships had invaded his kingdom, he sent messengers to ask these foreigners whether they brought peace or war. Before they reached the ships, they encountered Corineus and a party of armed men who had disembarked to hunt for game. They immediately asked Corineus by whose authority did he hunt in the king's forests, for no one should hunt there without the ruler's consent. Corineus answered contemptuously that no permission was necessary. This so infuriated Himbert, their leader, that he drew his bow and fired an arrow at the Trojan. Corineus dodged the missile and, charging at Himbert, struck him a fatal blow to the head. This so terrified the others that they fled back to Goffar and reported the death of Himbert. This news greatly displeased Goffar and, mustering a large army, he set out to exact revenge. Brutus ordered the women and children to take refuge in the ships and placed his men as a shield wall along the shore.

He joked with Corineus, 'This reminds me of the Trojan War, with us as the Greeks and the Aquitanians as the Trojans.'

Goffar attempted to break through the massed ranks of Trojans and destroy their ships, but the human wall stood firm and the slaughter lasted the whole day. Corineus was foremost in the battle, fending off the many blows hammered down upon his head and dealing out death to all who stood in his way. When his sword was shattered, he wielded his battle-axe, cleaving anyone who opposed him in two. Eventually the Aquitanians retreated in panic and Goffar fled the field, leaving Brutus the victor. As Brutus rejoiced, he reflected on the pivotal role Corineus had played in the battle. Brutus now marched his men throughout the land, mercilessly pillaging the towns and slaughtering the inhabitants. During this period, Goffar had sought refuge with the twelve kings of Gaul, who promised him that they would drive Brutus out of Aquitaine.

When Brutus reached the city of Tours, he learned that Goffar and the kings of Gaul, together with a vast number of armed men, had entered Aquitaine and were seeking to do battle with him. He immediately set about turning Tours into a fortified camp that would serve as a refuge for his men. When spies informed Goffar that Brutus was at Tours, he advanced by forced marches until he came face to face with his hated enemy.

He addressed his men with bitterness in his voice, 'These ignoble foreigners have laid waste my land. Arm yourselves my brave warriors and charge at their serried ranks. We shall seize these weaklings and carry them captive through my kingdom.'

Brutus, confident that his men were not weaklings, drew them up in battalions on the open plain before his camp and waited calmly for the Gauls to attack. When they did, it was with overwhelming numbers but the well disciplined Trojans held their ground and then advanced, throwing the enemy into confusion and panic. Goffar rallied his men and led them in another desperate charge that resulted in the slaughter of thousands; decapitated bodies and severed limbs covered ground awash with blood. At first the Trojans appeared to hold the advantage but, as is the case in many battles, the Gauls' superior numbers began to tell, and the Trojans were forced to seek refuge in their camp. Goffar immediately drew a ring of steel around the camp, thus trapping Brutus and his men.

That night, Corineus spoke urgently to Brutus, 'Goffar can now starve us into submission. I have a stratagem that will not only save our skins but, against the odds, will enable us to achieve an unlikely victory. Under cover of darkness, I and a battalion of my men will surreptitiously leave the camp and follow a secret path to the neighbouring wood where we will lie concealed. In the morning, your men will emerge from the camp and attack the enemy. Then, when the battle is at its most ferocious, I will attack them from the rear; their resulting confusion will more than cancel out the advantage they have in numbers.'

The plan worked perfectly and the Gauls fled the field, leaving the Trojans depleted in number but triumphant.

Brutus, while rejoicing in this triumph, realised that they could no longer stay in Aquitaine. Goffar would continue to harass them and they would never be able to live at peace with the Gauls. He therefore loaded his shops with the riches he had plundered and set sail once again for the promised island.'

When the Trojans next made landfall, they found themselves on an island blessed with bountiful fields, rivers teaming with fish and woods alive with game.

'Surely,' they said, 'this is the land the goddess Diana promised us. This is where we will make our home.'

There was, however, the small matter of the twelve-foot giants who considered it to be their home. Brutus and Corineus, deploying their battle hardened troops, soon drove the bewildered giants into the hills where they sought refuge in the caves. The Trojans then commenced building houses, ploughing the fields, fishing the rivers and hunting the game.

The giants had named the island Albion but, in a fit of hubris, Brutus changed the name to Briton and called the inhabitants Britons. Not to be outdone, Corineus named the region he ruled Cornwell and the people who lived there, Cornishmen.

Brutus had first landed on Albion at the port of Totnes, and he decided to give thanks to the gods by holding celebrations there in their honour. This was the occasion when the giants, led by Gogmagog, chose to attack them. The fighting was savage and many Britons were slain, but eventually the giants were defeated and the only one left alive was Gogmagog, a creature of frightening dimensions. Brutus was about to dispatch him with a blow of his axe, when Corineus intervened and expressed a desire to wrestle the monster. Brutus was astonished by the request and marvelled at the courage of Corineus. On being granted his wish, Corineus rushed at Gogmagog and lifted the startled giant onto his shoulders. Then, groaning under the weight, he staggered to the edge of the cliff and hurled the giant onto to the razor-sharp reefs below, where Gogmagog was cut into a thousand pieces and stained the sea with his blood. From that time on the place was known as Gogmagog's Leap.

Having exterminated the Giants, and secured his kingdom, Brutus undertook a royal progress through all the regions of his newly acquired realm looking for a suitable site on which to build his capital. He chose an area on the banks of the Thames and when the city rose on both sides of the river he named it Troia Nova.

For human beings, this island was a paradise, with its broad fields in which all kinds of crops were grown in their season, its woodlands which were alive with game, its orchards bursting with fruit and its rivers overflowing with fish. The Britons rejoiced in their good fortune and revered their king.

Brutus consummated his marriage to Ignoge and she gave him three sons. On his death they divided the land into three kingdoms that are now known as England, Wales and Scotland. Locrinus, the first born, inherited England; Kamber, the second son was given Wales while Albanactus, the youngest, received Scotland. That is why the first ruler of Wales was a descendent of a Trojan aristocrat.

Geoffrey of Monmouth (*c.*1100–51) was a British chronicler who became the Bishop of Asaph in 1152. He wrote *The History of the Kings of Britain* in which he traced the history of the Britons through 1900 years, from the legendary Brutus, great-grandson of the Trojan Aeneas, to King Cadwallader.

Further reading

Geoffrey of Monmouth (trans. Lewis Thorpe), *The History of the Kings of Britain* (1136).

Guest, Lady Charlotte, *The Mabinogion* (*c.*1838–49).

Keegan, John, *The Face of Battle* (1976).

Muntz, Hope, *The Golden Warrior* (1949).

Oldenbourgh, Zoé, *The Heirs of the Kingdom* (1971).

Prestwich, Michael, *The Three Edwards* (1979).

Runciman, Steven, *The History of the Crusades* (1951–4).

Smith, J. Beverly, *Llywelyn ap Gruffudd Prince of Wales* (1998).

Starkey, David, *Crown and Country* (2010).

Smurthwaite, David, *Battle Fields of Britain* (1984).

Waugh, W. T., *The English Historical Review*, 20 (1905).

Williams, Gwyn A., *Madoc: The Making of a Myth* (1980).

Williams, Gwyn A., *When was Wales?* (1985).

Williams, Peter G., *Owain Glyn Dŵr* (2011).

Acknowledgements

I must thank my editor, Eirian Jones, and the staff of Y Lolfa.

In writing a novel of this sort, I have had recourse to many experts and I take this opportunity to record my indebtedness.

My long-standing gratitude I give to my late wife Jean for the many joy-filled years we spent together.

Also by the author:

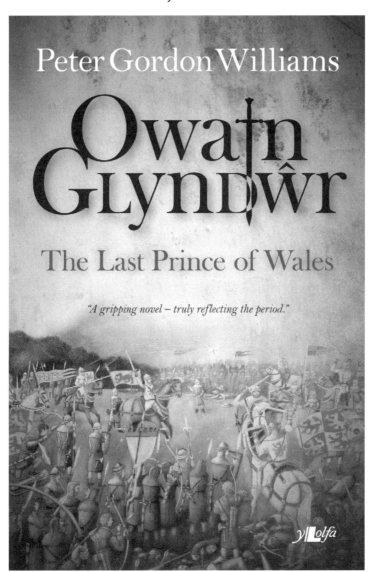

Peter Gordon Williams

Owain Glyndŵr

The Last Prince of Wales

"A gripping novel – truly reflecting the period."

y Lolfa

£7.95